Wren

Also by Lucy Hope

LUCY HOPE

First published in the UK in 2022 by Nosy Crow Ltd
The Crow's Nest, 14 Baden Place,
Crosby Row, London, SE1 1YW, UK

Nosy Crow Eireann
44 Orchard Grove, Kenmare,
Co Kerry, V93 FY22, Ireland

Nosy Crow and associated logos are trademarks and/or registered
trademarks of Nosy Crow Ltd

ISBN: 978 1 83994 723 0

A CIP catalogue record for this book will be available from
the British Library.

Printed and bound in the UK by Clays Ltd, Elcograf S.p.A
Typeset by Tiger Media

Papers used by Nosy Crow are made from wood grown in
sustainable forests

1 3 5 7 9 10 8 6 4 2

www.nosycrow.com

For my "favourite" children,
Hattie and Dylan

Chapter One

Anglesey, North Wales, 1870

The first time I heard my house sing, I might have missed it altogether had the gulls not fallen silent at precisely that moment. I was out by the boathouse, securing my coracle against the rising tide. I have never seen the water in the strait so high. Sweeping my hair from my eyes, I happened to look up just as the strange sound came again.

Our house often takes on a menacing air at that time

of the day, but there was something different about it that evening, something that sent a shiver down my spine. As I ran up through the gardens, past the towering rhododendrons and under the weeping willows, I had the most peculiar feeling that the house was watching me – tempting me, daring me to come home.

I swung back briefly to face the water, confused by the sudden silence of the gulls. There were none to be seen. The heaving mass of water was now almost invisible under a veil of low-slung dark cloud.

The song came again and I looked up, ignoring the wind whipping at my face. It seemed to be coming from somewhere up high, from the top of the tower, from behind the battlements. The mournful lament became so intense it took my breath away.

As I reached the wide hardstanding to the front of the house, the sun slipped behind the bridge and a wave of grey swept overhead; in this strange half-light, for just a moment, the house almost seemed to sigh.

I ran towards the back of the house, under the archway, past the stables. Perhaps it was nothing, just the wind whistling through the turrets. But a bird might be trapped on the roof; I couldn't ignore that. I flung the back door open, ran through the pantry, through the kitchens, past the sleeping cats lined up in front of the range and into the long corridor that leads to the main staircase. I didn't know what I was doing, but I knew I had to go up to the roof. If there was something trapped up there, I couldn't leave it to die.

As I ran up the stairs, the peculiar sound came again, more muffled now I was inside. It was long and low, and sent a shudder through my heart.

I reached the landing and tiptoed towards the small door that leads up to the attic. Easing the door open, I paused to listen.

Ignoring the little voice inside my head that told me to turn round, I stepped through the low doorway and climbed the steep, bare-boarded stairs up to the attic, using my hands to guide me. I reached the top of the stairs, wishing I'd thought to pull on a coat on my way up. A slim shaft of moonlight led me to the final flight of stairs that leads up to the roof. The boards under my feet vibrated as if someone nearby was beating a slow drum. With a pounding heart I climbed through the hatch and stepped out on to the flat lead-lined walkway that runs round the tower between the sloping roof to the left and the old battlements that overlook the waters of the strait. It was due to be a full moon that night, bringing with it a high spring tide. Waves were already lapping against our shingle beach, no doubt scooping up thousands of

3

pebbles and sweeping them out to sea.

A sudden shriek nearby made me jump, but it was just a family of passing gulls, squabbling somewhere out in the darkness.

Everything fell silent.

Even the waves seemed to still for a moment.

And then the song came again, loud and clear. This was no trapped bird, or other wild creature. The song was coming from all around, consuming me, its cool fingers clutching at me. It came from above and below, from the roof tiles, and the stone of the battlements.

I was alone on the roof of my house.

I was alone with the song of my house.

And then, with a great shudder, it just stopped. I stood motionless, suddenly feeling the intense cold, slowly coming to my senses. What was I doing up there? Had I lost my mind? I turned on my heels and fled along the walkway, tumbled through the little door, down the attic stairs, not caring one bit about the darkness as I raced to the safety of my room.

Chapter Two

That was three weeks ago now, and I haven't heard the noise since. I'd told Pa about it soon afterwards, but he'd laughed at me and said, as he always does, that I needed to rein in my overactive imagination.

He's already at the dining-room table when I come down for breakfast, hidden behind his newspaper. He lowers it just enough to see who has come in. Tudur is sitting by his side, in my usual seat.

"Good morning, Wren," Pa says. "Have you seen your aunt on your travels?"

"No," I say. "She's probably still getting dressed."

"At this time of the day?" he snaps.

I shrug. "I'm sure she's on her way." I take a seat, glancing at the serving table at the side of the room; it's empty apart from an oil lamp and a pair of large place mats. The door swings open and Alis comes in holding a steaming dish above her head. She's flanked by Gelert and Pelham, their snouts high as they inhale the scent of whatever she's carrying.

"Kippers," she says, rolling her eyes.

I jump up and grab hold of the dogs' collars, tugging them away from her, keeping hold of them until she's placed the dish at the back of the serving table. They sit next to me grudgingly, their wide eyes fixed on the dish, rivulets of drool dangling from their jowls.

"Someone needs to train that pair of oafs," Pa says. He looks at the door again. "Where *is* your aunt? Does she not realise what time it is?"

I've no idea why he thinks Aunty Efa's timekeeping is my responsibility. I blow out slowly, watching as a little white cloud forms in front of my face. The fire's been lit but it's still bitterly cold in here. It's dark too, darker than normal. The little lamp in the middle of the table encloses us in its dull yellow embrace, but the far end of the room is lost in darkness. Someone could be sitting in the window seat and we'd never know they were there.

A sudden explosion of noise from down the corridor makes us all jump. It's Aunty Efa. The distinctive clickety-clack of her wheelchair becomes more clamorous as she enters. She toots her horn – a harsh interruption to the silence of the room. Pa shudders as the acrid tang of steam and smoke reaches us. Aunty Efa's steam-powered wheelchair *is* an unusual sight, but it gave her freedom to get about after the accident without relying on other people, so who can complain if it's a bit noisy? She toots her horn again, looking at Pa pointedly, and manoeuvres herself into place across the table from me. Steam belches from beneath her wheels as she comes to a standstill.

"Is breakfast ready?" she says, glancing at the serving table.

Tudur wafts her smoke away with a hand and pretends to cough, his eyes slipping to Pa, as if looking for his approval.

"I only just brought it in," Alis says. "It's still piping hot."

"That is not the point," Pa says, folding up his newspaper. "Breakfast is always served at eight, and it is now five past."

Aunty Efa ignores him, instead nodding a brisk thank-you to Alis as she plonks a plate of kippers and eggs in front of her before serving the rest of us. Pa slides his spectacles into their silk case and tucks in. I look at Aunty Efa surreptitiously. Her hair is piled high on top of her head and held in place with an elaborate arrangement of wire and lace and something that looks like an oily rag. She notices me looking at her. "It's the latest fashion," she says, patting her hair. "From Paris, would you believe?"

"You look like a true Parisian lady," I say. "Very stylish."

Pa appraises her in the way he often does, eyebrows high, chin raised slightly. "You appear to have brought a quantity of engine oil with you to breakfast, dear."

Aunty Efa taps the rag that's entwined about her hair like a serpent. "And so indeed I have. Thank you for bringing it to my attention, Wigbert."

"You'll start a fashion for it!" I say. "Everyone in Beaumaris will be wearing them soon. You'll see."

She laughs. She probably came to breakfast dressed like this just to annoy him. He's too busy pulling bones from his fish to notice how she's narrowing her eyes at him.

I'm desperate to get out of here and on to the water.

I heard a rare bird was spotted out there yesterday, somewhere near Church Island. If I take my notebook with me, I might even get close enough to do a quick sketch.

"I'm going out in my coracle this morning," I say, to break the silence more than anything else.

"No, you are not," Pa replies. He hates me going out on the water, especially at this time of year, but he doesn't normally try to stop me.

"Yes, I am." I try to sound firm. I don't want to explain again how important it is to me, and that being out on the water is the best way to stop thinking about Ma.

"No, you are not, Wren, because I have arranged for Mrs Hughes from the institute to come over and work on your embroidery with you."

"I don't want to work on my embroidery, Pa!" I say. "It's a waste of time. And I'm no good at it."

"That is because you spend too much time on the water, when you should be honing your needlework skills."

I glare at him. I'll make sure I'm nowhere near the house when Mrs Hughes arrives. She's always telling me my fingers are too rough from all the time I spend outside, that I'm too impatient, that I'll never be a "proper young lady" if I can't learn to sit still for hours at a time. And her breath smells of cabbages.

"You're too like your blasted mother," Pa hisses.

"Don't call her that," I cry. "She was brilliant, not blasted."

"Oh, so brilliant she went and got herself killed. What kind of mother does that, eh?"

I ball my fists and sink my fingernails into my palms. Even Tudur looks upset with Pa now. "How can you say that?" I shout.

"The problem is, Wren, you're going down the same path and, like her, you seem incapable of accepting your limitations." His face is flushed. He knows he's gone too far.

"She knew what she was doing," Aunty Efa hisses at Pa. "It's *you* who has the problem in that department, Wigbert."

Pa starts picking at the fish skin left on his plate, his brow furrowed.

"But you don't have to be like her, you know, Wren," Aunty Efa says. "One daredevil in the family was more than enough, considering what happened." She takes a sip of coffee. "And that sea breeze does horrible things to your hair."

I shouldn't have expected her to be on my side. All she's interested in is where her next dress is coming from or whether I'll embarrass her in front of her friends. "I just want to look for a bird," I whisper.

Pa sighs. "Well, if you kill yourself, it'll be your fault. You know what those currents are like."

"I'm always careful," I say. I want to shout that if I wasn't careful every time I went out on the water, I'd be dead like Ma, but I bite my lip, slide my chair out and run from the room before he tries to stop me.

"So we'll cancel Mrs Hughes then, shall we?" Aunty Efa calls after me.

I don't reply.

On my way back to my room I glance at the correspondence tray, hoping something might have arrived from France, but it's empty apart from a small silver toothpick and a pair of spectacles.

It's choppier out on the water than I expected, and I struggle to control my coracle as I scud about on the grey waters in the shadow of the bridge. My boat bucks and twists and I move my body from side to side to keep it steady. The currents are even more vicious than normal today, and I paddle hard to keep a safe distance from the Swellies, the most dangerous part of this stretch of water. The cold air helps to calm my mind. I know I'm like my ma – Pa tells me often enough, as if that's a bad thing. But she was clever and kind and talked to me about everything – about her dreams, and her huge, unwieldy ideas. Pa said once, after returning from a lock-in at the Royal Oak, that he thought he'd have been able to "break her in" like a horse, after my grandfather, the local doctor, had given up on her, but Ma was not to be licked into shape by any man.

I scan the waves with my binoculars, hoping to spot the bird everyone's been talking about. The red-necked grebe, hardly ever seen in these parts, especially in winter, was spotted just last week, according to Alis, but today there isn't a bird in sight. Even the gulls are hiding.

Eventually I give up; it's just too cold. Pa won't ask me how I got on. His only interest in birds is whether they fly slowly enough for him to shoot them or what type of display case will best suit their plumage.

It takes far longer than I expected to get back to the shore. High waves smack against the side of my boat, some leaping inside, threatening to drag my coracle and me down. I bale out water as quickly as it comes in, all the while paddling hard to get home.

I'm close to the shore when I spot a pile of white and grey feathers bobbing on the surface of the water nearby. I paddle towards it against the current, unsure what it might be. As I get closer, I realise it's a gull, tangled up in a piece of fishing net and flapping desperately as it attempts to extract itself from its prison. "It's all right," I call. "I'll help you."

I ease my boat alongside it and lean out, but a current snatches it away from me. I stretch out a tiny bit further; I can't leave it to die. My frozen fingers almost make contact with the bird, but just as I'm close enough to grab it, it bobs out of reach. Muttering under my breath, I push my paddle into the water and follow it. I draw alongside it once more, but just as I reach out to lift it from the water, a wave slaps the side of my coracle. Not expecting the sudden movement, I topple out into the icy sea. Gasping for breath and inadvertently sucking salt water up into my nostrils, I swim towards the creature, and eventually manage to grab hold of it. I quickly spin round and, struggling against the weight of my heavy dress, swim back towards my boat, reaching it just as my feet touch rocky ground. I stagger out of the water, the bird dangling from my wrist, and haul my boat out, swearing like a fisherman.

As soon as I'm back on the beach, I collapse in a heavy, soggy heap and with shaking, numb fingers set about untangling the creature. Using my teeth and a foot to tear at the netting, I eventually set the bird free. It doesn't hang about to say thank you, but simply lifts itself up with powerful wings, and is soon lost in the mass of low clouds.

Knowing I can't sit here for long in my wet clothes, I drag my boat up the beach, my skirts clinging to my legs. The sky is turning to a deep charcoal, suggesting a storm is on its way. I quickly secure my coracle and waddle up through the garden towards the house. The wind whistles through the battlements at the top of the tower; it's making a peculiar sound, like someone playing a tune through gapped teeth. I run under the archway to the side of the house, through the yard, wrapping my shawl tightly round my shoulders, and burst in through the back door.

Mrs Edwards, the cook, glances up as I pass. She's at the butcher's block, in a food-stained apron, hacking at a piece of meat with a cleaver. I've no idea what creature it once was but guess it's now something to do with supper.

"Hello, Wren," she says, looking me up and down with her eyebrows raised. I keep to the other side of the table as I pass, so she doesn't notice how drenched I am.

"Hello, Mrs Edwards," I reply. "Is that supper?"

"Not tonight's. For tomorrow. Fresh pheasant, it is. Shot by your pa. It's been hanging in the pantry for a good two weeks. Should be nice and tender."

"Hmm, delicious," I say, shuddering inwardly at the sight of the shining red flesh being tossed into a pile of bite-sized pieces.

"Not known as much of a shot normally, is he, your pa?" she says, her eyes gleaming. "Better make sure he knows how much you appreciate it!"

"I will," I say, briefly warming my legs in front of the range, before sloshing out of the kitchen.

Chapter Three

I wake up to a bright-blue sky, so decide to go out on the water again to try to find the grebe before it disappears forever. Not wanting to get drenched again like yesterday, I find some suitable-looking clothing hanging from a hook in the justice room. I peel off my dress after spending far too much time fiddling around with its tiny buttons, and step into a pair of voluminous overtrousers. I hoist them up as high as they'll go and tighten the buckles over my shoulders. I tug on an old jumper, which probably belongs to Pa, and tie an oilskin sou'wester to my head.

I creep as quietly as possible in oversized rubber boots along the corridor that snakes past Pa's study, already sweating under all my layers. The door's shut; he's probably entertaining one of his friends in there, or sharing his philosophical ponderings with Tudur. I have to get out before the tide goes out too far so pick up speed. I'm almost at the end of the corridor when I hear the study door swing open behind me.

I glance backwards and immediately regret it.

Pa's at the study door with Tudur by his side. Tudur's smirking, like he always does when he senses trouble. He's dressed in a smaller version of Pa's suit and his hair is parted in exactly the same place. If he had a monocle in an eye and a smattering of facial hair, you'd think he was just a shrunken version of Pa. I narrow my eyes at him, wanting more than anything to wipe the irritating smile from his face.

Pa's looking at me in horror. "What are you doing, Wren?" he says, as if I'm the most perplexing creature on earth, "and what do you think you're wearing?"

I look down at myself and shrug. I think it's fairly obvious what I'm wearing.

"If you had a clay pipe dangling from your lip and a basket on your head, I wouldn't be able to tell you apart from some sort of fishergirl!"

"I'm just on my way out, Pa," I say, edging down the corridor away from him. "I need to get my coracle out."

"That blasted coracle," he snaps. "I don't know what your mother was thinking, giving you such a ridiculous little boat."

"It isn't ridiculous," I hiss. "It's my boat and I love it." I smear my sweating palms on my rubbery overtrousers.

He shakes his head. "It's embarrassing, Wren. But this –" he waves a hand, indicating my clothes – "proves my point rather well. Come into the office, will you. We have visitors."

"But I'll miss the tide," I groan.

"That is not my problem."

I shuffle after him into the study. I've only taken two steps into the room when I freeze.

"Pa?" I whisper, my heart pounding.

Two tall, thin, expensively dressed men are standing side by side near the furthest window, looking out towards the water, their hands clasped behind their backs. But even from this distance, and with their backs turned, I know exactly who they are. What is Pa doing letting *them* into our house?

18

Pa takes a seat at his desk, a self-satisfied look on his face.

The men turn to me. I've never been this close to them before, but I've seen them enough times around Menai Bridge and Beaumaris. My heart begins to pound. Something makes me worry this is all about me.

They step towards me and I take a step back towards the door.

"Don't be rude, Wren, come and say hello to our guests," Pa says. He's actually smiling, as if he's enjoying this.

I allow my eyes to dart in the men's direction. They're not smiling like Pa; their thin lips are set in rigid lines. Their pale, watery eyes are almost lost in deep, bony hollows set high in their sallow cheeks. But still I feel the intense scrutiny of their gaze.

"After your outburst at breakfast yesterday, and your little episode on the water," Pa says, "I have decided to take action." He sees the look on my face. "Yes, yes, of course I heard what happened. I do know what's going on in my house, however much you try to sneak about like some sort of vagrant."

My heart begins to pound. What does he mean by this? These are the Aireys. They run the infamous and much-feared Anglesey Institution for the Re-education of Young Women, or A.I.R.E.Y.W. for short, housed in a wing at Beaumaris Gaol. Girls from all over Wales and beyond are sent there by fathers or brothers unable to control them. It's said that anyone who is released, and many never are, emerge back into the world shadows of their former selves.

I concentrate on the painting behind Pa's desk and try to stay calm. I can't imagine why he'd want to own such a thing. A soldier in shining armour on a white horse is driving a lance deep into the belly of a small dragon. The doomed creature is writhing on the rocky ground, dark-red blood spilling from its wound. I feel for the beast's plight.

Pa picks up a yellowing leaflet from his desk. "It says here," he says, "that the school excels in the cooling of hot heads, teaching young women how to submit to authority, and supporting them to banish their demons from within."

"Pa?" I whisper, stepping towards him. This must be some sort of joke. Maybe he's just trying to frighten me.

"I think you'll be suitably amused by the daily activities they offer." He runs his finger down the pamphlet. "What do we have here? Ah, yes, here it is. It's very varied, Wren. I'm sure you'll find plenty to amuse yourself. There's poetry, needlework, flower arranging, cookery classes, learning to listen carefully and empathetically." He scans the leaflet. "And all the usual things about deportment, eating properly and learning one's place – that sort of thing."

Pa took me to visit this place a year ago. I never knew why as he didn't mention it again. I wondered at the time if it was a warning – that he was trying to frighten me into behaving how he'd like me to. I've never forgotten the faces of the girls as they sat in neat rows, their heads low. There was nothing remotely amusing about it.

"You'll be begging for an embroidery lesson with Mrs Hughes in no time at all," he says, laughing.

The Aireys remain motionless, their eyes not leaving me. A shiver runs down my spine. We've all heard the rumours about the beatings and the punishments – girls being forced to wear undergarments lined with giant hogweed, causing blisters and burns that last for weeks.

Tudur has taken a seat at the desk by the window and watches me with a small smile on his lips, his chin resting on both hands, like a child at a puppet show.

I stare at the oil painting behind Pa's desk, blinking back tears as one of the two men hands Pa a document for him to sign. Pa looks up at me, pen poised. "They have made a place available for you, as a special favour, so you'll be able to start on the twenty-first of December!"

He tells me this as if I'll be pleased to be shipped off to an institution like that just before Christmas! I feel numb, but my mind is racing. I won't let this happen. Pa won't make me go. He knows what it's like. And the Aireys don't just run a terrible institution. It's also rumoured they're involved in all sorts of illegal schemes. Pa would never willingly do business with them, would he?

A loud tooting makes us all jump. It's Aunty Efa arriving with a screech of brakes at Pa's office door. Pa's face does that thing it always does when Aunty Efa's around; the vein that runs from the outside edge of his right eyebrow up to his hairline pops out and jiggles about like a little worm beneath his pale skin. His upper lip trembles, as if he's trying to suppress a snarl. The Aireys start muttering to each other.

Pa quickly signs the paperwork and passes it back to them.

I run to Aunty Efa and help squeeze her giant wicker wheelchair into the room, leaning into her ear as I do so. "You have to help me," I hiss.

I'm briefly distracted by her appearance, which even by her standards is dramatic. She's dressed in a green gown, her flame-red hair arranged in a foot-high mound on top of her head with three peaks at the top.

22

Yellow velvet ribbons are entwined within the arrangement, like streams of gold. Ma would have described it as a *feat of engineering*. The overall effect is slightly marred by the little smuts splattered about her face, a side effect of having a steam engine and coal scuttle attached to the back of your wheelchair. Pa's always grumbling about it. Always has, ever since she adapted it, and constantly complains about the soot it creates. He says living in our house is like living down a coal mine, which of course is nonsense, and he wouldn't know anyway as he's never been down one. I'm just happy she can get about and do useful things like rescue me from Pa.

"Before we were interrupted," he says slowly through tight lips, "we were discussing important business with Wren. I'd be grateful if you would allow us to resume our conversation."

Aunty Efa looks at the Aireys and narrows her eyes. "I apologise for the interruption, Wigbert, but I too have important business to discuss with Wren." She presses on a small brass lever on the side of her chair and the scuttle tips up, allowing a quantity of coal to rattle down into her furnace. Steam swirls around her ankles, rising in a great plume until she's lost within a cloud of white smoke.

My mind is racing as I work out what to do. There's no way I'm going to allow Pa to lock me up in that institution with those men, just because I like being outside. It doesn't make any sense. I glance around – at Pa, perched all pompous and prim at his precious desk, at the seemingly lifeless Aireys with their threadbare heads and elongated, hairy ears, and my irritating little brother, all slowly becoming lost in Aunty Efa's smoke. Pa pulls a handkerchief from his top pocket and coughs into it. Tudur soon disappears entirely. The Aireys are making strange gurgling sounds, with one muttering "this is most unacceptable" to the other.

"I need to borrow Wren," Aunty Efa says sharply. "I need her help with something."

"You will do no such thing," Pa hisses, his forehead vein wriggling like a serpent. "I'd appreciate it if you left us to our family business."

Aunty Efa trundles towards Pa and parks in front of his desk. I take a small step towards the door.

"I'm her family too, Wigbert, and I have my own business to discuss with her. *Yours* will have to wait."

One of the Aireys steps towards Pa. "You are proving your point rather well," he says. "It's clear to us that you have no control whatsoever over your family."

Pa is practically puce now. "Oh, just go," he says. "Go

and deal with whatever matters are so pressing they prevent me making arrangements for my daughter's education."

I spin round and follow Aunty Efa out of the room. I don't know where we're going, but at this moment I really don't care.

Aunty Efa travels at full pelt through the house, down long, twisting corridors, past closed doors. With the racket from her steam engine it's impossible to hear what she's saying, so I just trot behind her, my mind swirling like the waters of the Swellies. Three weeks! Pa wants to send me to the most notorious institution in Wales in three weeks' time just because I wanted to take my coracle out, rather than do needlework! Ma would never have let him try something like this. I smear angry tears away with the sleeve of my jumper, suddenly feeling ridiculous for being dressed in these clothes. They won't have helped.

I realise we must be heading to Ma's old workshop as we race past a series of closed doors. If *I* was going to the workshop, I'd go outside, through the yard and past the stables, but this is better for Aunty Efa. The floor is a bit uneven, but it's tiled, making it safe for a fast-moving, steam-powered wheelchair. As I follow my aunt, I wonder if she sometimes feels as trapped as me. I can't imagine she likes living with Pa any more than I do, but maybe she doesn't have anywhere else to go either.

The corridor eventually becomes so narrow you can touch both sides, and on a whim I run my fingers along the dark stone walls. They're cold and wet and slippery.

We sometimes have visitors to the house – tourists intrigued by its unusual design – and they always come down here. Some people compare the corridors that weave about the building to the capillaries and arteries that run around a body, delivering blood to its vital organs. Some of the corridors are even slightly rounded, adding to this impression – the house has very few angles or straight lines. I'm used to it so it doesn't feel that strange.

We're close to the furnace room now, the cavernous space at the centre of the house that holds the giant firepit. Medwyn, a boy about my age, has the task of keeping this fire alight, ensuring our house remains warmish, our water hot and the kitchen ranges burning.

As we pass the open doorway, I glance in. He's in there, shovelling coal on to the firepit in the middle of the room. I poke my head in and wave. He nods curtly then turns away. We used to play together all the time when we were little, but he doesn't have much to do with me these days. Not since his pa died and he took over his job as our stoker. I get the impression he doesn't think much of my family, or me.

I chase after Aunty Efa down the narrowing corridor. I don't like this part of the house; it gives me the creeps. Eventually the corridor splits into two. We take the right fork and head for the door at the end. Aunty Efa drives straight into it. The door crashes open and we burst out into the yard.

"Ah, that's better," she says, inhaling the chill air, reducing her speed as she rattles over a cobbled area of ground, avoiding piles of horse dung and muddy ruts.

"Shall I push you?" I say.

"Goodness, no. What's the point in all this if I have to rely on other people?"

I shrug. "But you were rescuing me from Pa, weren't you? You've heard what he has planned?"

"I have, and I can't do anything to stop him, I'm afraid. His mind is made up. But what I do object to is him inviting that pair of unsavoury individuals into the house. They stink of mothballs, Wren! And I do not appreciate the way they look at me." She shudders.

I bite my tongue. I should have known better than to think she'd help me.

"No, my dear, I need your assistance with something else."

I stare at her open-mouthed.

"I've had a delivery this morning and I'd like your help getting it up to my room. It's in the workshop."

I shuffle after her into Ma's old workshop, my heart heavy with the realisation that no one can do anything to stop Pa.

Chapter Four

We find the dogs in their usual place in front of the brazier. They still come here every day, even after all this time. The two of them are stretched out next to each other, their legs tangled together, making it difficult to see which paw belongs to which dog. For a moment I imagine Ma sitting at her desk, diagrams spread everywhere, a dog resting a soft chin on her lap.

I feel Ma here more than anywhere else. I'll never

forget the last time I saw her. Her hair was wilder than ever that day, her face smeared with some sort of black goo. She was in her leather spatterdashes and a pair of Pa's mud-splattered hunting boots. I was always so proud of her. So proud she was the sort of person who didn't give two hoots what anyone thought of her. She'd wiggled an oily finger at me and grinned. "Care for a hug?" she'd said.

I remember how I stopped her touching me, because of her oily hands.

Aunty Efa is busy unwrapping a new mannequin. I wriggle down between the dogs and run my fingers along one of Gelert's velvety ears. He presses his soft nose into my face.

Eventually I get up and take a seat at Ma's old workbench. I flick through one of her notebooks, remembering how she used to talk all the time about her dream of flying like a bird. She built a flying machine after hearing about a Frenchman called Le Bris who'd done just that. Being Ma, she'd used her own design, but she must have done something wrong because, unlike Le Bris who was able to stay up for several minutes, she and Aunty Efa had lifted up into the air and then fallen to earth like a stone. Ma was killed and Aunty Efa broke her spine, and our lives were changed forever. A couple of months ago, an idea had started to form in my head that I couldn't shake out, so I wrote to Le Bris asking about his *L'Albatros artificiel*, or artificial albatross. It was a silly idea really. And of course he hasn't replied. He's too busy being a famous inventor to bother with a twelve-year-old girl trapped on a little island in North Wales, but still I dream that one day I might fly up into the sky, swooping and soaring over the waters of the strait, like Ma never got to do. I know it won't bring her back, but it's a longing too strong to ignore.

I glance over at Aunty Efa's latest mannequin. She'll have had it specially made for her in London, no doubt; she says she doesn't like the headless, limbless bodies normally used to display dresses. This disturbingly life-like mannequin still has a few strips of brown paper wrapped round its midriff and bust area. "Let's keep this paper here for now," she says, "in case we encounter any of our menfolk on the way up. Save their blushes, eh?"

"Do you have a dress in mind for it?" I say, even though I'm not particularly interested.

"Of course! A new gown arrived just yesterday. The timing is perfect."

I place Ma's notes back on the workbench and together we lug the mannequin through the house.

With its arched brows, red lips and elaborate hairstyle, it almost looks alive. I help steady it as Aunty Efa wheels herself on to the lift and hop on just as we start rising up to the first floor.

I don't go to her bedroom that often so am surprised to find her mannequin collection has grown since I was last in here. It's a huge room with three windows overlooking the water, but still it feels cluttered, with dozens of lifeless figures all dressed, as if about to go out, in Aunty Efa's gowns. A pair of mannequins, clad in russet and umber tones, are sitting at a low table by the fireside, as if enjoying afternoon tea. A further three stand at each window, taking in the view, and one sits in a chair by the bedside table as if poised to read to her. Aunty Efa does go out a lot, and is well known for her smart clothes, but even so I can't understand anyone needing this many dresses. I make an excuse to go as soon as I've helped her fit her latest gown over the new mannequin.

That evening I come to dinner wearing one of my frilliest dresses. I decided after leaving Aunty Efa that I might try to be a model daughter for now, at least until I've worked out a better plan. Pa does change his mind all the time, so it's worth doing my best not to annoy him. I've just spent a miserable hour being detangled and defrizzed by Megan, Aunty Efa's maid, allowing my hair to be piled up into an arrangement not dissimilar to hers. The dress is stiff and uncomfortable with a wide sash round the waist and a huge bow at the front – all adding to the general impression of me belonging more in a cake-shop window than a dining room.

Pa doesn't comment on my appearance. In fact, he hardly seems to notice me at all.

As soon as we start eating, we're briefly interrupted by a low rumble from beneath the floor. A light breeze flits about the room like a sprite, cooling my cheeks, making the lamps flicker. We all feel it, but no one comments because it's such a regular occurrence. Pa said a while ago that the house was built on soft ground, which is why it moves more than a normal house and why we keep getting spontaneous cracks appearing in the walls.

No one mentions the Aireys' visit, not even Tudur. It's almost as if it didn't happen, but perhaps Pa's just trying to avoid an argument. A little part of me still hopes it was just one of his jokes, designed to frighten me into behaving how he'd like me to.

Pa and Aunty Efa start discussing Tudur and his latest piece of schoolwork. Apparently it's on something to do with mathematics. Pa says Mr Thomas, our tutor, has described him a "prodigy" and mentions it at least twice in the conversation, which makes me bristle inside. Mr Thomas suggested Pa should send Tudur's findings to the editor of *The Times* for publication. Tudur has that annoying expression on his face – the one that Pa does when he's pleased with himself about something, but which looks even more ridiculous on a ten-year-old boy. Pa never talks about my schoolwork.

He suddenly swings to face me.

"We didn't finish our little chat, did we, Wren, after your aunt smoked out my study. I had something else I wanted to discuss with you."

I stare at my lap, not wanting to meet his eyes.

"But not to worry. I've decided it can be a surprise. That'll be much more fun."

A surprise does not sound "fun" at all, and will probably make it even more difficult to get out of. I look at Aunty Efa desperately.

"Oh, I love surprises," she says, clapping her hands together, not even looking at me.

Pa smirks. "It can be an early Christmas present for you, Wren!"

"I don't want an early Christmas present," I growl.

Pa laughs and Tudur joins in. "Oh, you will, my dear,"

Pa says. "It will be your moment to shine."

A knot returns to my belly like an unwanted house guest. I want to shout at Pa, but Aunty Efa shoots me a warning glance. I bite my lip instead.

We eat pudding in silence, interrupted only by the gentle hiss of Aunty Efa's engine and the creaks and groans of the house. My mind is whirring with unsettling thoughts – about the institution, and now Pa's surprise. He's not going to change his mind.

I need to think of an escape plan.

As soon as we're done, I run from the room and sprint towards the stairs. But something on the hall table catches my eye and I skid to a halt. It's a letter. This definitely wasn't there earlier. I pick it up and turn it over. It's addressed to Monsieur W. Cecil-Lloyd. I'd assume it was for Pa but for the block of unusual stamps taking up a large part of the front of the envelope. I pick it up and turn it over. On the back, in neat handwriting, is the name and address of the sender. My heart misses a beat. It's from Monsieur Le Bris in France. I hadn't told him I wasn't a man when I wrote to him. I'd signed my letter W. Cecil-Lloyd, so he must have just made that assumption. I slide it inside my dress and head to my room where I'll be able to read it without interruption.

I climb into bed, take my letter out and open it carefully, my heart pounding. Ma would have loved to have received a letter from Le Bris! I wonder if she's watching me now.

After a short salutation, Monsieur Le Bris, goes on to describe in tiny, perfectly formed handwriting how he built his *L'Albatros artificiel*. In addition to his letter, written in excellent English, he includes a series of carefully folded hand-drawn diagrams, illustrating how he was able to make his "bird" lift up into the air and bring it back down to earth without killing himself.

I can't imagine what it must be like to fly higher than a house, to look down on the world from above, like a god. The thought of it makes my heart soar. I don't blame Ma for trying.

I breathlessly turn over page after page of tissue-thin paper. Le Bris talks of how he glided like an albatross in flight, using pockets of air called thermals and updraughts to stay in the sky. He explains how if you fly through a thermal, it lifts you up even higher, like someone blowing beneath a feather. He goes on to discuss a phenomenon called *aspiration*, which explains how the shape of a wing helps you lift up into the sky. He says the shape of the wing is everything. I examine the sketch he's included. It's of a huge bird-like contraption, its wings outstretched, perched on a pair of large, spindly wheels. I breathlessly flick through the pages, barely able to believe that this remarkable man has taken the time to write to me. I suspect he might not have had he realised I was "just a girl", but I don't dwell on that thought.

Eventually I fold the letter up, return it to its envelope, blow my candle out and slide further under my eiderdown.

People were quick to pass judgement about Ma and Aunty Efa after the accident. The newspapers pontificated on the audacity of a pair of women attempting something so ambitious. Pa read every article and sighed and swore a lot before screwing them all up and hurling them into the drawing-room fire. Some columnists even remarked on what the tragedy said about a man who allowed his womenfolk such freedom. Pa raged about those ones the most. Some of the kinder pieces merely suggested that if people had been meant to fly, they'd arrive in this world with wings attached.

I think Aunty Efa eventually began to believe everything written about her, and over the last two years has transformed herself from a slightly reluctant daredevil into who she is now. But I know she still goes down to the workshop from time to time, to have a tinker with an old project, or look through some notes or ideas, or just to conceal an extravagant delivery.

With all the excitement of the letter, I'd almost forgotten about Pa's plans for me. My stomach lurches. There's no way he's going to get me through the doors of that place. I'll just have to keep showing him I'm the perfect daughter while I work on my escape plan.

In the morning I climb out of bed and tiptoe to the window, clutching my eiderdown like a cape. I hook my curtains back and look out over the water. The gulls are going about their early-morning business, skimming the waves in little groups before soaring up and away from each other in a dozen different directions. I blow on the window, watching as my warm breath turns to steam and settles on the glass panes, briefly obscuring my view of the sea.

A prickle runs up my spine as I'm suddenly overwhelmed by a feeling that someone's standing just behind me. I freeze, not daring to move, barely daring to breathe. I feel a slightness of breath as if another person is close by, just behind my shoulder, enthralled, like me, by the spectacle of the birds on the sparkling water and the snow-capped mountains beyond. I know I'm imagining it, but the feeling is so overwhelming I can't help but spin round, hoping she's found a way to come to me.

But of course it's just me in here, with my overactive imagination and my silly hopeful heart. But just a little part of me believes that somehow she knows.

Chapter Five

I soon discover what Pa has planned for me. His *little surprise*, as he called it. He summoned me to his study just before tea and told me we have an appointment with a special visitor tonight at St Tysilio's church on the island. He insisted I dress "respectably" and then watched me like a hawk until we were ready to leave. Aunty Efa is away, visiting a friend in Caernarfon. I wonder if the timing is a coincidence. Pa'd tried to reassure me that it's just a simple history talk, but seeing the way his eyes slipped away from me as he spoke has made me worry there's far more to it than that. I even begin to worry if it has something to do with his plans for me and the institution.

We walk from the house to the church in a short procession made up of Pa, holding a torch to light our way, then me, then Tudur. It's bitter out here. A light dusting of frost on the ground suggests the night will be even colder. My mind is whirring so much I can barely think straight as I glance about, looking for an opportunity to run away. As if reading my mind, Pa falls to my side and takes my arm, his fingers gripping me so tightly I cry out.

He's looking so smug for a moment I even let myself believe it's all nothing – just him playing some sort of cruel game.

We cross the narrow causeway that leads to Church Island and I shuffle with a sinking heart towards the low door of the ancient little church. Pa pushes it open and ushers Tudur and me inside. We're met with a sea of cigar breath and expectant shining faces. Men with ruddy noses, bushy side whiskers and bulging eyes sit elbow to elbow with women in tall feathered hats perched on top of elaborate hair arrangements. Every seat is taken apart from our pew at the front. I glance anxiously at Pa, my palms clammy despite the cold. He refuses to meet my eyes.

A man, not the vicar, is standing at the front of the church, near the altar. It's difficult to see his face as he has a russet-coloured cowl pulled up over his head, casting his face into shadow. The light from a tall candle behind him gives the impression he's glowing slightly.

We walk in a line down the aisle, past the scrutiny of the candlelit congregation. My cheeks burn under their gaze. I walk past a row of grand-looking old ladies sitting upright in stiff crinolines. Pa holds his head high, seeming to enjoy the stir we're causing.

We reach the front pew, and after a small kerfuffle, with Pa deciding who should sit where, we sit down. The room falls silent.

The man at the front lowers his hood to a collective gasp, followed by awkward shuffling and whispers of outrage behind me.

I look at Pa.

I want to shout at him. What is he thinking?

The man turns to me, his pale eyes scrutinising my face, a small twitch playing at the corner of his lips. He has the distinctive hollow, age-ravaged cheeks and ice-blue eyes of one of the Aireys. My stomach clenches.

Like a rabbit in a trap, I glance about desperately, glaring at Pa, then pleading at him with my eyes. He's sitting with his legs crossed, his hands resting on his thighs, an entirely unreadable expression on his face; even Tudur isn't imitating him for once. The atmosphere in the church has changed entirely. I surreptitiously glance behind me and am faced with a sea of anxious eyes.

The man begins to speak. His voice is thin and reedy and sets my teeth on edge. My heart is thumping so loudly, I almost don't register any of his words to begin with. Instead I stare at my boots, not wanting to have any eye contact with him, but still feeling the burn of his gaze on the top of my head like a hot hand.

Eventually I realise he's talking about my family and our "esteemed" ancestors. He talks of the chieftain who fought bravely to keep the invading English forces out of Wales in the time of Edward I, and whose descendants built the house in which we live. He talks of the importance of the house to the history of Anglesey, and even to all of North Wales, and that it must be preserved "at all costs".

For a second or two I almost dare to believe this isn't all about me, that I've been imagining things, that Pa just wanted me to show some interest in the family history. But I still don't understand why he invited this man here, and dragged Tudur and me along.

I cast a glance at the man, to subtly scrutinise his craggy features, but as I do so his eyes swivel back to me. I instantly look down again.

"Wren," he says.

Pa nudges my arm. "Look up when you're being spoken to," he hisses.

I draw my eyes from my boots and, with my head hanging low, meet his gaze.

Our eyes lock.

The scratching of shoes on stone floor and the rustling of taffeta skirts ceases.

And it seems that, just at that moment in the little church, not one person dares to breathe.

Is this all part of Pa's attempt to change me? Is that what this is all about? Pa wanting to humiliate me in front of everyone from the island so I become the person he wants me to be?

The man bends stiffly and picks up a leather pouch that until now has been lying at the foot of the lectern. He reaches into it with long pale fingers, and with a theatrical flourish pulls out a skull. He says it was found recently in St Margaret's church, not far from here. "This," he says, "is irrefutable evidence of the lineage of the Cecil-Lloyds. *This* is the skull of Gruffudd ap

Bleddyn ap Llewelyn."

He tosses the pouch to the floor, holds the skull up high in one hand, and with the other beckons to me. I shrink into my seat. What has any of this got to do with me? I ball my fists in case he tries to come too close.

"This distinctive jaw is evident in the latest generation of Cecil-Lloyds. This –" he looks at me as if wondering how best to describe me – "this *girl* here," he says, almost spitting out the word, as if it is the worst sort of insult, "has inherited this distinctive feature."

I bury my chin into my dress, fighting back tears. Even Tudur isn't smirking any more. I glare at Pa. How can he allow this man to do this?

"Here, child," the man whispers, clicking his fingers.

I refuse to look up.

"Wren Cecil-Lloyd," he says slowly, spitting out my name as if every syllable appals him. "Now."

I desperately look to Pa for help, but he stands up, grabs me by my elbow and manoeuvres me up to the lectern. The straight-backed ladies and their immaculate daughters are sitting slack-jawed as they watch the spectacle.

Pa returns to his seat, leaving me trembling and alone.

"Now, face me," he says in his brittle voice, "so our audience may have a clear view. That's right, child, now chin up." His face is too close to mine, his breath cool and musty on my cheek.

I want to run down the aisle and disappear into the night, but instead I stand numbly and do as he tells me. I raise my chin, blinking away tears.

He holds the monstrous object up in front of my face, its empty eye sockets staring back at me. "The evidence is irrefutable!" he croaks. "See how the jaw of Gruffudd takes on this particular curve?"

I glare into his icy eyes. I want to snatch the skull from him and smash it into his head, but just at that moment a crash from the back of the church distracts us all, including the Airey, and a blast of air fills the room, followed by the arrival of dozens of gulls. Soon the church is full of the creatures, flapping, swooping and dive-bombing the ladies' hats and splatting on the shoulders of the top-hatted men.

The Airey hisses something under his breath, as he swipes at the birds now attacking him, tugging at his cowl, pecking at the hairy protrusions sprouting from his ears. Swearing, he slides his precious skull back into its drawstring bag and tucks it under his arm. He stalks to the far end of the church and disappears through a low door, slamming it behind him.

The audience is now on its feet; the ladies are fighting

off the gulls snatching at their feathers and lace-entwined up-dos with white-gloved hands, the men swatting the birds away from their sideburns with silk handkerchiefs. They jostle out of the room in a clatter of clicking heels, swirling feathers and cross words.

A boy fights his way into the church through the crowd, carrying a small wooden pail. It's Medwyn from the furnace room. He waves his bucket in the air, lets out a low whistle, and the birds cease their flapping and fly in a great white squawking mass back to the door and disappear off into the night.

I follow them out, pushing my way through the stragglers, and without really thinking what I'm doing run towards the water.

I head towards the bridge and reach the small beach that sits in its shadow. I tear off my boots, hoist up my skirts, sprint across the dark sand and plough into the water, desperate to be engulfed by it. How could Pa do that to me? Did he really think I'd be pleased to have my face compared to a skull? Did he think I'd be proud, like he clearly is? I want to submerge myself in the icy water, to let it slip over my head, to take away the burning heat still consuming my cheeks.

The shock of the cold water brings me to my senses. What am I doing? The water is so cold it could kill me if

I stay in too long. I drag myself and my heavy skirts back to the shore. When I reach the beach I sink on to the wet sand and hold my head in my hands and begin to shiver uncontrollably.

A voice interrupts my misery. "Are you all right?"

I turn round and glare into the darkness, mortified that whoever it is must have witnessed the spectacle of me hurling myself into the sea. It's Medwyn.

"I am, now I'm out of that place," I say.

He sinks on to the sand next to me and sits with his arms wrapped round his knees, looking across the water towards the mountains. "I thought you'd appreciate the distraction just now, you know."

"Thank you," I say, "for rescuing me. It was you, wasn't it? With the gulls? I didn't know you could do that."

"There's a lot you don't know about me," he replies. "A bit dramatic, I know, but it was all I could think of to get you out of there. What was your pa up to, letting an Airey near you?"

I shrug. "He doesn't care about that. Why would he? He's happy for me to be sent off to their horrible institution, so why should this be any different?"

"He's doing what?" Medwyn looks shocked. "He must know what the place is like."

48

"Presumably," I mutter, fighting back tears.

A crunch of feet on wet, grainy sand nearby startles me and I spin round, expecting to see Pa. But it's just Medwyn's aunt, come looking for him. Even though she's only *his* aunt, everyone round here calls her Aunty Dilys.

"All right, Wren?" she says, standing over me, her hands on her hips.

I nod. "I am now."

She looks at me and then at Medwyn, then back to me again, chewing on her lip as if trying to work something out but she doesn't say anything else.

My shivering is starting to take hold of my whole body, but I don't want to go home. "Were they your birds?" I say, turning back to Medwyn. It feels like a stupid question. Does anyone own birds?

"Well, they're not mine exactly. They just sometimes do as I say, if there's a bucket of worms on offer."

I bury my hands in the sand, hoping to somehow warm them up.

"I have to say, I think you look nothing like that skull."

"Why, thank you. Not even the eye sockets? Don't I have its eye sockets?"

He laughs. "Nor the protruding brow!"

"Well, that's a relief."

We fall into silence for a moment. Aunty Dilys is staring up at the bridge.

"And anyway, should that make you special?" he says quietly. "If you did happen to have the jaw of someone who died hundreds of years ago? Should that make you better than the rest of us?"

"I didn't say it did!" I say, suddenly feeling ashamed all over again. "I don't know why Pa did that. You know I'm not like him. But thank you for the disturbance."

"My pleasure," he says, touching the peak of his cap.

"You take care, young Wren," Aunty Dilys says.

I haul myself up heavily; my skirts are now caked in sand as well as soaked in sea water. "I'd better get home, before someone sends out a search party."

I stumble home, wondering how I'm going to deal with Pa when I get back, but a little part of me is hopeful that Medwyn might want to be friends again, just like we were when we were little. The thought sends a bubble of happiness through my stupid, lonely heart.

I drag myself back towards the house, raging with Pa. Why didn't he make Tudur go up to the front of the church instead of me? But then Tudur doesn't have what Pa refers to as "the family jaw". And I'm also sure this is all linked to Pa's feelings about my unseemly behaviour.

Was he just trying to make a point? Was this all about making me feel even smaller than I already do?

I walk up the lawn towards the house, my body numb with cold. It seems to be emitting a most peculiar light. There's always a lamp or two left burning through the night, giving the windows the look of yellow eyes silently watching the strait and the mountains beyond. But I've never seen it look like this. A warm, orange light is oozing out through all the little cracks that run like thread veins across the old stonework, giving the house the appearance of a cracked egg lit up from the inside.

Aunty Efa's mannequins look down on me, their noses slightly raised, as I pass beneath her bedroom windows.

I squelch towards the house, ignoring the strange pricking sensation running down the back of my neck. I stumble and trip on something hidden in the long grass. I right myself, but then the ground beneath my feet rises up in front of me like a low wave, before flattening out again. I tumble forward and land heavily on my knees. Muttering under my breath, and hearing Pa's voice in my head about my stupid overactive imagination, and worried that the cold water might have affected my mind, I pick myself back up again, glancing about nervously. The lawn has returned to normal.

But then a deep groan, like the sound of an animal in

pain, fills the air. It's coming from somewhere high up in my house, and for one terrible moment, I fear it's about to collapse.

The house shudders, and then the strangest sound begins. It's a tune – deep and low, and very like the noise I heard a few weeks ago.

I freeze.

And then the sound seems to pass above my head and drift across the water like a low cloud, towards the mountains, and soon is gone.

A tall, shadowy figure comes into view, carrying a torch.

It's Pa.

"You stupid child," he shouts, stumbling towards me. "Look at the state of you! Did you fall into the water again? Did you take your blasted boat out in the middle of the night?"

"I needed to cool down," I snap. "How could you do that to me, Pa? How could you humiliate me like that?"

"Oh, Wren, you're so dramatic sometimes. It was just a bit of fun."

"It was not a bit of fun!" I hiss. "It was awful and embarrassing." I glare at him. How could he possibly think I'd be pleased to have that man breathing his musty breath in my face, comparing me to someone who died hundreds of years ago?

"Well, I agree it didn't go quite to plan, but that was because that stupid boy turned up."

I ignore him. I don't want to give him an excuse to turn on Medwyn. I often wonder if Pa's the reason he stays away from me. "And did you just hear that?" I shout, waving up at the house. "You can't say *that* didn't just happen!"

"Did I hear what, dear?"

He's definitely looking shifty now.

"I heard that strange sound coming from the house again," I say. "The one I told you about last time, the one you said was a *figment of my imagination*!" I shout the last bit at him.

"Are you quite well?" Pa says, reaching out as if to test the temperature of my forehead.

"Of course I am!" I say, backing away from him. "It's your ears I'm worried about. How could you not have heard that?"

"I think perhaps you're delusional," Pa says, trying to put an arm round my shoulder, but I shake him off.

"I am not delusional," I hiss.

He grabs my elbow and marches me into the house, complaining about the state of my dress with every step.

"And this is why you're beyond help," he says,

ushering me in through the back door. "This is why I've had to resort to extreme measures with your education. It hurts me more than it hurts you to send you there, Wren. You must remember that. This is your fault, not mine!"

I want to throw myself at him and thump him over and over on his chest, but I'm suddenly overwhelmed by exhaustion, and instead follow him like a lamb up to my room. I run into my bedroom, slam the door behind me, and after much fiddling about with tiny buttons and cold fingers, hurl my dress across the room and climb into bed.

I lie awake for hours, my teeth chattering, unable to warm myself up, my rage ebbing and flowing, all the while listening to the low grumbling and strange beat of my house, trying and failing to force the events of the evening out of my mind.

Chapter Six

I'm still chilled to my bones when I wake up. It must be late as the sun is streaming into my room through the still-closed curtains, illuminating a million dust particles dancing about in the air. I keep the covers pulled up to my nose as I churn over yesterday's events in my mind. I'm still upset with Pa, but my rage has been tempered by the memory of Medwyn and the thing he did with the gulls, and how he and his aunt came to find me afterwards, as if they knew where I'd be.

There's a quiet knock at the door and a tendril of smoke slips underneath it and creeps up the side of my bed.

"Are you there, Wren?"

"No," I reply.

The door creaks open and Aunty Efa puffs into the room, her wheels rattling on the floorboards. She's dressed in a beige poplin travelling dress, and smells of the sea. Her hair has been roughly piled up on top of her head and wedged beneath a hat.

"I heard about last night," she says. "I got home as quickly as I could."

I don't trust myself to speak.

"I don't know what he was thinking. I've tried to find him this morning but I suspect he's hiding. Are you all right?"

It's not like her to take my side. I eye her suspiciously. "Not really," I whisper.

"He clearly didn't think it through; you know what he's like. He was probably persuaded it was a good idea by someone, and didn't for a moment consider your feelings."

Of course, being an adult, she's bound to defend him, but I know I'll never be able to forgive him.

"And I heard what happened afterwards. I know you were upset, but what on earth were you doing going for a midnight swim? You might have drowned, Wren!"

"I wouldn't have cared if I did. And it would be all his fault."

She rolls her eyes and places a cool hand on my forehead. "We must hope you don't develop a fever. I'll have a word with him when I find him."

I often wish she was more like Ma. More concerned about people than possessions and appearances. But Aunty Efa can be kind sometimes, if it suits her.

"I hope *he* got splatted on by one of those birds," I say. "I hope they splatted all over his stupid cravat."

Aunty Efa laughs and I pull the covers up to my nose.

"And while I go to seek out your pa, could you do a little job for me?"

I look at her suspiciously. "What?"

"Can you go out and find Emrys? Mrs Edwards wants to know if he'd like to eat tonight."

"Is he back?" I say, trying to remember when I last saw him. It must have been weeks, if not months ago.

She nods. "I believe so."

"He'll want to know what's on offer."

"Roast duck, it is. In an orange sauce."

"Do you think he'll eat that?"

57

"Who knows? Probably not, but Mrs Edwards is worried about him. She said he's looking positively skeletal."

"He's always a bit willowy," I say, "but I'll ask him." Already I'm wondering if this might be an opportunity to question him about the strange noises coming from the tower. If he's back at the ice house, he might have heard something.

No one really knows who Emrys is. He comes and goes as he pleases. Some say he's an old Druid. Others with more fanciful inclinations say he's some sort of wizard. I think he's just an old man who quite enjoys the air of mystery that surrounds him. "Do you know what potatoes she's doing?" I say, knowing Emrys will almost certainly ask about that.

"Not dauphinoise. Mrs Edwards wouldn't have offered if it was dauphinoise."

"An abhorrence in potato form," I say. "Why ruin a perfectly acceptable vegetable with the juice of the udder!"

Aunty Efa laughs. "Oh, Wren, I'd forgotten he said that!"

She leaves me feeling much better than when she came in, and I lie in bed listening as she chugs off down the corridor, calls for the lift and then waits until the noisy contraption arrives to take her back downstairs.

I find Emrys sitting cross-legged on frosty grass in his usual long, white robes by the entrance to the ice house. His eyes are closed and his pale hands are resting on his knees. His bare feet are an unhealthy shade of grey-blue. I worry he might be dead, but as I get closer, I spot the shallow rise and fall of his chest. His leather sandals have been placed neatly next to him, alongside a sturdy-looking stick.

"Hello, Emrys," I say.

He appears not to hear me.

"Um, hello," I say, after standing over him awkwardly for a moment, resisting the temptation to nudge him with my boot.

He opens his eyes slowly and looks up at me.

"Ah, young Wren of the house, how may I help you?"

I wrap my cloak round myself and stamp my feet. How can he sit outside like this, dressed in such thin clothes? "Well, Mrs Edwards was asking if you would like supper tonight."

"And do you mind me asking what she's cooking?"

"I think it's duck," I say, "in an orange sauce."

He sighs and stares off into the distance, perhaps expecting the gulls to answer my question. A sudden gust blows a strand of long white hair across his cheeks and he sweeps it away with a pale, sinewy arm.

Eventually he turns back to me. "The problem is, I don't think I could possibly eat such a dish, no matter how delicious the orange sauce. Without risking offending Mrs Edwards, I can't help thinking that duck is better served with a plum sauce."

He's been known to return dishes that are not to his liking, often with suggestions for how Mrs Edwards might improve her cooking, but she never seems to mind. She's ferocious with everyone else, but never with Emrys.

"So, shall I say you don't want the duck?"

"No, no, let's not be too hasty," he says, shaking his head. "Tell Mrs Edwards that if she doesn't mind rustling up a plum sauce, I'll gratefully accept her offer." He squints up at me. "You do all look after me so well." His eyes are almost lost under ancient, heavy lids, but they're still as bright as periwinkles. I suspect they're the sort of eyes that miss nothing.

I shift my weight from one foot to the other, wondering how to broach the subject of my house.

"Spit it out, child," he says. "I've been on this earth long enough to know when someone has something on their mind."

I briefly explain about the strange song I've heard coming from the top of the tower.

He eases himself up to standing, using his stick to help him. "There are those that have the ears to listen, and there are those that choose not to hear," he says, his robes billowing around his legs like sails.

"So, have you heard it?"

"'Tis the lament of the lost and alone," he whispers almost to himself.

"What does that mean?" I say, trying not to sound impatient. "Who's lost and alone?"

"'Tis a cry for freedom," he adds.

And with that he bends down, picks up his sandals, hoists up his gown and tiptoes gracefully through the long grass towards the ice house. Without even saying goodbye he disappears inside and slams the door behind him.

I stand there for a moment, wondering what on earth he was just talking about.

As I head to the kitchen to report back to Mrs Edwards, I pass Pa's study and hear raised voices coming from inside. I press my ear to the door. The dominant voice is that of Aunty Efa and it sounds like she's giving Pa a good telling-off. The door is off the latch so I open it just a couple of inches and peer inside. Pa is sitting behind his desk and Aunty Efa is facing him in her chair.

"How could you do such a thing?" she hisses. "Hasn't the girl been through enough already?"

Pa says something incomprehensible.

"But that's just ridiculous," she says. "Surely you know what those people are like. Your job is to protect her, not stick her directly in the path of one of the Aireys."

"Well, I didn't know he'd bring along the skull," Pa says petulantly.

"And you arranged it knowing full well I was going to be away," Aunty Efa says.

Pa mumbles something I can't hear.

"With Bronwen gone of course I'm going to stand up for her. You certainly don't seem to be doing so!"

"She just needs to know who she is, what her duty is and where her loyalties lie," Pa snaps back.

"What her duty is? What are you talking about, you silly little man? She's a twelve-year-old girl. Her only 'duty', as you call it, is to come to terms with the death of her mother!"

I don't think I've ever heard Aunty Efa stand up for me. I wonder if she took a blow to her head on the way home from Caernarfon.

"That was two years ago!" Pa shouts. "She needs to

move on and think about her responsibilities with the house. I felt she needed a little reminder of who she is in case she ever has to make a decision, should anything happen to me, or Tudur."

"She's Wren," my aunt hisses. "And she isn't going to have to make any decisions in the near future. She's just a girl, Wigbert."

I bristle about being described as "just a girl".

"But she isn't just a girl, is she? She has the blood of Gruffudd ap Bleddyn ap Llewelyn coursing through her veins." The way Pa's talking about me now makes me sound like some sort of bodily organ. "Tudur takes pride in that knowledge, and has vowed to protect this house at whatever cost. Wren, on the other hand, has not been taking her responsibilities seriously." He sounds more and more preposterous with every word he speaks. I'm only twelve. What is he expecting me to do? "And why do you care so much about her all of a sudden?" he snaps.

"It was very inconvenient," Aunty Efa says so quietly I have to strain my ears to hear her. "Aunty Dilys was so worried about what happened she took it on herself to send a message, urging me to come home. She said you'd done something terrible. I thought there was a problem with the house, Wigbert! And I ruined a perfectly good pair of trousers riding through the damned rain."

"Well, I'm sorry if I inconvenienced you, but I had to do something to rein her in. Put her back in her place."

"Like you did with Bronwen?" Aunty Efa laughs. "Oh yes, you did an excellent job of reining her in, didn't you!"

"I won't let history repeat itself," Pa says slowly through tight lips.

"And are you really still going ahead with your plans for the institution?"

"Indeed I am."

"Well, I think you're being cruel. And the fact that you're sending her there is like admitting to the whole of Anglesey that you can't control your own daughter. Have you thought about that?"

"It's my house and she's my daughter, and I will do what I like with her," Pa says. "This is none of your business, Efa."

"Well, I think it's just about the worst idea you've ever had," she says.

I don't want to listen to any more of this. I have no idea what Pa wants me to do about the house, or why he thinks I have a special responsibility just because I have a determined chin. And I'm not a builder. I can't fix the cracks in the walls. I leave them to it, sort of grateful to Aunty Efa for standing up for me, even though she described me as "just a girl", and head out through the kitchens towards the workshop. I have more important things to do than worry about what's going on inside Pa's head. Finally I'll have the chance to look through the letter again in conjunction with Ma's plans. Maybe I might now be able to make sense of them.

As I run across the yard, I realise I might actually be able to build a flying machine. I could prove everyone wrong about Ma. I could show Pa I'm much more than an unruly girl. And if I did manage to build something that flies like a bird, I might even be able to escape all of this.

Chapter Seven

When I get to the workshop I light the brazier, climb into Ma's chair and pull her old blanket over my knees. My mind whizzing, I lift down one of Ma's old notebooks from the shelf above the workbench, hoping to find some empty pages to write on. I flick through them, one by one, feeling the familiar knot rising in my throat whenever I see Ma's big, elaborate handwriting. I swallow the lump away crossly. Some of the notebooks contain random scribbles, thoughts and ideas, and others have pages filled with neat-looking lists of parts, technical calculations and costings. I find one with only half its pages filled with notes. Notes about Ma's greatest invention. The invention that killed her and broke Aunty Efa's spine. I hold it to my chest and breathe her in for a moment, feeling her close to me.

"What would you say about me now, Ma," I whisper, "with a letter from a famous Frenchman explaining how to build a flying machine?" I think she'd be proud of me. She might even describe me as *a chip off the old block*, like she used to when I was little and built giant structures with the wooden blocks that had been spurned by Tudur.

I decide this will be the perfect notebook for the job.

Ma was always writing lists. It was the first thing she did when she started a new project. I decide to do the same. I know I should probably think more about this. I'm always rushing headlong into things without thinking them through, but Ma always said when an idea comes calling, you just have to grab it with both hands and see where it takes you. I decide I'll start with a list and see where that takes me.

I turn to the first empty page in the book, lick my pencil and begin writing a list of the items I'll need to build an artificial bird based on the information in the Frenchman's letter:

2 x large wheels

A wooden crate (for the undercarriage)

A small boat (for the hull)

Lightweight wooden batons for the wings (quantity to be decided)

10 yards of silk fabric

Plumage (feathers)

Glue and staples (for attaching fabric to the batons)

A length of rope (check length required)

Cord for the controls (quantity to be decided)

Pulleys

Suitable clothing for flying

Monsieur Le Bris explained in his letter how his "artificial bird" had two parts – "the undercarriage", which comprised two wheels and a framework for supporting the "bird" when it was still on the ground, and then the "bird" itself, which was made up of a hull with giant wings strapped to either side of it and a tail for steering. He said that when the wings caught the air, the "bird" part of the contraption would separate from the wheels and framework, leaving them behind as it soared up into the sky. The "bird" then became a sort of flying boat, and could only be landed on water.

It doesn't take long to find Aunty Efa's old wheelchair wheels, from before she converted her chair to steam. I find them leaning against the wall of the storeroom next to the workshop. They're quite spindly things, with slim, bamboo spokes. I press down on one with all my weight; I think it should be robust enough.

The next item on my list is a crate for the undercarriage. I find one that looks about the right size, but full of apples, in the fruit store. I tip the apples into the adjacent half-empty box of pears, turn the crate upside down, and jump up and down on it for a bit, hoping it will be strong enough to take the weight of the "artificial bird" and me.

Soon I've gathered most of the things I need. I realise with a heavy heart that my coracle will be the best thing for the main body of the flying machine. It isn't the perfect shape, but I'm sure I'll be able to adapt it; it's just something to sit in, after all, and I know I fit into it. As soon as the project is over, I'll be able to return it to the water. I lug it up from the boathouse. It isn't that heavy, but it's an awkward shape and I realise I probably look like a giant snail as I run up through the gardens holding it over my head. I drag it into the workshop and place it next to the other parts. Le Bris built a sort of deep canoe that he stood up in to fly his machine. My coracle should work just as well. It's light and sturdy. I'll just have to sit down in it when I fly, that's all.

My next job is to find a length of rope. Le Bris used rope to attach his artificial bird to the horse and cart that towed him up into the air. He says he released the rope as soon as he was airborne. I'll have to think carefully about the knot I choose as it'll have to be released quickly, so I don't end up lifting whoever is towing me up into the air too! I eventually find a suitable length of rope curled up like a snake under Ma's desk.

I look through my list, and tick off the items I've gathered so far, my belly bubbling with excitement.

A gentle knock at the door draws my attention away from the list. The door opens, and a boy with a mop of dark, curly hair steps into the workshop. It's Medwyn. He looks as surprised to see me as I am him.

"I've just come to light the brazier for the dogs," he says, his eyes searching the room, "but I can see you've already done that." He hovers in the doorway as if waiting for me to invite him in.

I cringe as I remember how he last saw me shivering in my soaking dress on the dark beach. "Thanks for helping me, you know, the other night," I mumble.

He shrugs. "Would have done it for anyone in a similar situation. Can I come in?"

I nod too eagerly, and he steps into the room and tosses another log on to the fire. "Aren't you freezing?"

"Not really."

"You need to keep it stoked, see, if you want it to keep throwing out the heat."

"I know how to keep a fire going," I say, probably too frostily.

He peers at the papers on the workbench. "And what do you have there? Are you an inventor like your ma?"

"I'd like to be. Would you like to see?" I do feel I can trust him. "These are plans for an artificial bird, a flying machine, one big enough to hold a person!"

His eyes widen as I hand him the letter.

"It's from a Frenchman called Le Bris. He looked at the wings of an albatross and worked out how it flew, and applied the same principles to his invention."

Medwyn examines the diagram in detail. I pull Ma's blanket more tightly round me and watch him as he reads.

"What do you think?" I say when he passes it back to me. "You seem to know quite a lot about birds. Do you think this could work?"

He looks a little uncomfortable. "I guess *he's* already

71

proved it does, but what about what happened with your ma?"

"I'll just do it differently," I say, aware I'm probably jutting my chin out at him. I don't tell him that the small, fanciful part of me hopes she might be watching from wherever she is now. "Would you like to help? I've already starting gathering the bits and pieces I'll need."

"What, help you build an artificial bird?" He scratches his head but he's smiling.

I nod. "Look – it's all here. I've got half the things I need already." I'm even more excited about it now, thinking I might be able to do it with Medwyn, that it might help us be friends again. I hand him the notebook. "Look, I've ticked some items off already!"

"Would you be able to find all these other things?" he says, scanning the list.

"I'm sure we can rustle up what we need." I try to sound more confident than I feel. "And I know where I can get hold of the fabric for covering the wings. There are boxes of old dresses down in the cellar. I'm sure they'd do. And I think there are some old feathers there too."

"Aunty Dilys might be able to help with the wooden batons for the wings. She knows everyone on the island.

I'll ask her. She seems to like you, so you never know."
His eyes are shining. "And I'm good with a needle. I
know how to stitch a sail. There'll be a lot of stitching
involved!"

I nod, grinning.

We spend the next hour reading and re-reading the
letter and making notes.

"Can you imagine what it would feel like to fly like a
bird?" I whisper.

"I think it would be terrifying!"

"But exhilarating! I could fly away," I whisper, my
heart thumping at the thought. "I could fly up over the
mountains and far away, where no one would ever be
able to find me! Away from Pa and his stupid plans."

Medwyn looks at me. "I'm sure he isn't really planning
to send you to that place."

I shrug. "You don't know him as well as I do."

Chapter Eight

My mind is alive with thoughts about building a flying machine as we wait for Aunty Efa to come in for dinner, and I realise I've been so distracted I've hardly thought about my impending imprisonment all day. Pa keeps glancing at his pocket watch. Supper is already out on the side table. He gets up and fusses about with the lamp, trying to eke out a bigger flame. Tudur is sitting opposite Pa, his hair perfectly oiled, back straight, his face freshly scrubbed. The dogs are stretched out in front of the fire, warming their paws.

After a while we hear the rumble of Aunty Efa's wheelchair, and she arrives, at least ten minutes late, in her usual flurry of smoke and steam. Eventually the air clears, revealing the most alarming item attached to her head. It takes me a moment to realise what it is. Pa and Tudur look at her in horror.

"Good God, Efa, what are you doing wearing a hat to dinner?" Pa says. "What do you think this is? A tea room?"

She raises her eyebrows at him. "Don't you like it, dear?"

"I think it's an abhorrence!" he says. "You look like some sort of –" he searches for the right word – "some sort of … cancan dancer!"

"Oh, don't be ridiculous. You've clearly never seen a cancan dancer!"

Pa sniffs and looks away.

I'm horrified by her hat, but for other reasons. I know the style is the latest fashion, but this is abominable. The hat, pinned to her perfectly arranged coiffeur, is made entirely from birds – dead birds. They look to me like hummingbirds, and have been arranged like flowers on an elaborate framework of wires and springs. Seeing me watching her, she wiggles her head. The birds jiggle about as if they're alive.

"Isn't it clever!" she says, shaking her head again. "I thought it might cheer you up."

"Are they real?" I ask.

"Of course! From Madame Guerin in London!"

"But they're birds, Aunty Efa!"

She looks at me as if I'm stupid. "Yes…"

"But shouldn't they be alive and flying, rather than dead and attached to your hat?"

"Oh, Wren, you and your silly ideas!" She rolls her eyes and takes a slurp of red wine. "Wigbert, explain to your daughter about fashion, will you? The importance of making an impression."

Pa looks at her carefully. "The point is, Efa, it is not done to wear a hat to dinner!"

Aunty Efa snorts.

"I think it suits you," Tudur says, smirking at me.

I glare at my obsequious little brother. He probably wants something from her. He couldn't give two figs about fashion.

"Well, I just think birds shouldn't end up on people's hats," I say.

"What a childish notion," she says, looking a little offended, before turning to Pa. "And I'm very aware it isn't smart to wear a hat for dinner, but it arrived this afternoon and I couldn't resist trying it on, and you know what a nuisance it is to take these things off."

Pa shakes his head and clicks his fingers at Alis, who is swiftly by his side, placing a plate of food in front of him. "And why is my duck coated in plum sauce?" he says, staring at his plate. "Mrs Edwards knows I don't like plum sauce."

Alis shrugs. "It's just what she gave me to bring in."

I realise it's going to be one of those dinners, with everyone tetchy and cross with each other.

"Have you remembered I have rehearsals tonight?" Pa says to no one in particular, scraping the sauce off his duck.

"Are they coming here?" Tudur says, his face lighting up. He loves showing off to Pa's singing group.

"No, we're meeting at St Tysilio's."

Tudur's face falls.

"And how are the rehearsals going?" Aunty Efa asks.

"Rather well," Pa says. "I've been working on my lower range and projection. Everyone is extremely impressed."

"Oh, jolly good," Aunty Efa says, chewing on a mouthful of duck.

"Of course, Adelina Patti predicted this."

"What are you talking about now?" Aunty Efa says.

"You know – Adelina Patti, the opera singer. Remember how she told me I had great potential as a tenor. At Covent Garden. Have you all forgotten?"

"I believe she might have been trying to get rid of you, dear," Aunty Efa says. "I seem to remember she was trying to escape the hordes in the lobby at the time."

"Oh, don't be ridiculous. She simply recognised a fellow songbird."

Aunty Efa raises her eyebrows as she takes another sip of wine but doesn't say any more on the subject. "And have you been to inspect our latest crack?" she asks.

"I'll have a look in the morning," Pa says. "When it's light."

"I think we should knock it all down and start again," she says. "This is the most ridiculous house."

"This house will be preserved at all costs," Pa says through tight lips.

"But how can we keep preserving it if it insists on falling apart at the seams?"

"We just have to make sure it doesn't," Pa hisses. "And I have external help now, as you know, which will help to fund the repairs."

"Your new friends, the Aireys?" I mutter. "What do

they know about buildings? Don't they just lock children up?"

"Oh, don't start all that again," Pa says.

I glare at him but say nothing.

"You may be surprised to know," he adds, "that they, unlike some people in this room, realise the importance of history."

"But why are they so interested in *our* house?"

Pa rolls his eyes as if I'm being unbelievably stupid. "Because your ancestor, Gruffudd ap Bleddyn ap Llewelyn, lost his life in a battle to keep the English king out of this land, and they're very grateful for his efforts. And you should be proud of that too." He shouts the last bit at me.

I bite my tongue. It's a pointless argument and he won't change his mind. But, whatever he says, I know I'm just Wren, nothing to do with the people who came before, even if I do have their determined chin.

Chapter Nine

In the morning I decide to go and see what useful things I can find in the cellar, certain there's a box of feathers down there, and some trunks of old dresses too. I step carefully down the steep stone stairs that lead to the network of low-ceilinged rooms beneath the house. It's strangely warm down here, warmer than you'd expect for a cellar. I reach the bottom of the stairs and enter the first room, holding my lamp high to cast as much light as possible over the gloom.

I tiptoe over fallen timbers that criss-cross the earthen floor, glancing about, looking for anything that might be useful for the flying machine. I haven't been able to stop thinking about it, and how Medwyn seems as excited as me!

I reach the next room in our subterranean maze and find it even warmer in here. I wonder if I'm directly below the furnace room, but it's impossible to tell.

A quiet thud nearby startles me and I spin round, my eyes stretched wide, searching the darkness. Realising it's one of the old timbers coming away from the ceiling, I crouch down and touch the ancient wood. It crumbles under my fingertips. I glance up anxiously, wondering how safe it is down here.

I step hesitantly into the next room, making a mental note of my bearings so I can find my way out. This room contains even more boxes and crates than the previous one.

A large leather trunk squats moodily in a corner of the room by the side of a box of crimson ostrich feathers. I hold my lamp above the trunk, creak the lid open, pluck out a sheet of old tissue paper and toss it to the floor. Underneath I find a pile of neatly folded, ancient gowns. The one at the top looks like it's made from silk, and in this light appears to be a dark shade of grey. I place my lamp on the floor and pull it from the trunk. But, as I lift it up to examine it, it falls apart in my hands. I watch in dismay as slender fragments of ancient silk float to the floor like butterfly wings.

The floor begins to tremble, and, surprised by the unexpected movement, I fall to my knees. The strange vibration eventually subsides, but I remain on all fours, my heart pounding.

The temperature rises and a most peculiar sound begins – a slow, rhythmic pounding that seems to echo the beat of my heart. But it isn't a noise exactly. It's more of a sensation than anything else. Strangely I don't feel alone down here, or as frightened as perhaps I should.

The floor feels warm to the touch and I sink my fingers into the soft earth. I stay like this for some time until the pounding ceases. I have no idea what I'm doing, but it feels right, and a sense of calm slowly descends.

Heat rises around me and I smell woodsmoke. Another unusual aroma becomes apparent; something I can't identify. It isn't unpleasant, and almost has a tinge of roasting meat about it, mixed with cloves and other spices.

The temperature plummets and the pungent odour disappears. My lamp has been extinguished, as if someone, or something, blew it out.

A nearby door slams.

A low rumble makes me freeze.

It's the sound of men's voices.

I leap up and shove everything back into the trunk, close the lid and crawl into the narrow gap between it and the wall.

Maybe Pa has some builders in to look at the cracks, but why would he bring them down here? The voices are getting louder, suggesting an argument has broken out. The slightly higher pitched of the three voices belongs to Pa.

I peek round the side of the trunk just as three men come into the room. Pa and two others. I don't recognise the other two immediately in the dim light of Pa's lamp, but when they speak, their scratchy tones are immediately recognisable.

Pa's looking flustered, his normally slick hair is wild, his cheeks flushed. He walks over to the other side of the room and pulls a small shelving unit to one side, revealing a low door behind it. The two men stand just behind him, their backs to me. They're tall, much taller than Pa. Both have only a few strands of fine, white hair clinging to their pale scalps.

What is Pa doing down here with the Aireys?

I watch with a mixture of interest and fear as he pulls out a bunch of keys from his trouser pocket, selects a large key, slides it into the lock and jiggles it about for a while until the door eventually clicks open.

The three men peer through the door into the darkness beyond. It seems that no one has the courage to step through the door first.

"And how is it?" one of the Aireys creaks.

"Very much alive," Pa replies. "And growing. Every time it has a growth spurt, it causes another damned crack in the masonry. I'm doing my best to shore it up, but there's only so much an old building like this can take. It's costing me a fortune."

What are they talking about? Is there something, or someone, imprisoned beneath my house?

"And is the Druid still feeding it?"

"I'm assuming so, but I don't understand how."

"Slippery as an eel, that one," one of the Aireys says.

They must be talking about Emrys!

"You need to do something about him. This can't continue."

"Do not tell me what to do in my own house," Pa snaps.

"Well, if you don't, then we will," one of the Aireys says darkly.

"Good luck with that!" Pa says, stooping to pass under the door lintel and into the darkness. "You clearly know nothing about him."

The Aireys follow Pa through the door. I crawl out of my hiding place and without thinking follow them into a low narrow tunnel.

I stay as close behind them as I dare, desperate to hear the remainder of their conversation. What on earth are they talking about? Is there something living and growing under my house? Is Pa engaged in some sort of business with the Aireys, beyond trying to send me to their institution?

"Did you get it valued?" Pa says.

I strain my ears to hear the response to his question. "Yes, but it's not worth as much as we hoped," replies one of the Aireys. "Old Evans at the mine said we'd get a guinea at the most for it. It can't go through the official channels, see, so that affects its value. So a third each, as we agreed."

"And there are plenty more where that one came from!" the other laughs.

They reach another low door and stand close behind Pa, breathing down his neck, as he fights with another lock.

"But any future haul will result in a fifty-fifty split,"

Pa says.

"We are comfortable with a third each," one of the men says.

"Of course you blooming would be," Pa snaps, spinning round to face him. "But that is not what we agreed."

"Well, would you like us to share your little secret with all of Anglesey?" the closest Airey says, pressing his face up to Pa's. "We'll happily pay the relevant authorities a visit if you choose not to do business with us any more."

"No, no, no," Pa says, tapping the man's arm. "You don't need to do that. It's just I'm having to share my third with my blasted sister-in-law. She knows something's going on, and has agreed to keep her nose out for the sake of a new dress here and there, so this is costing me more than it is you. And I'm having to fork out for the repairs. So a half guinea my way would be more appropriate, don't you think?" He smiles obsequiously from one Airey to the other.

I gasp as I absorb his words. Aunty Efa is taking money from Pa.

"It's a third each, or *everyone* gets to hear all your little secrets."

Pa shakes his head and turns back to the door, swearing under his breath. The Aireys are blackmailing

Pa, but he doesn't seem that innocent either.

"His lordship should be more careful who he shares his secrets with after a skinful of claret," one of the Aireys says, laughing.

"You promised it would be between us!" Pa says, still fighting with the door lock.

"And so it is, so long as the figures remain satisfactory," the other Airey hisses.

"And you are not to touch the old man," Pa says.

"We will do as we please with the Druid," the Airey closest to him says. "He's an inconvenience we could do without."

They're making threats about Emrys! How could anyone wish to harm such a gentle, old soul?

Finally the door opens with a loud clunk and Pa steps through the doorway into a dimly lit room beyond. The Aireys follow him and I take a tentative step towards the door, not sure if I really want to know what lies beyond it. I should probably turn and flee, but I need to know what Pa's up to.

The temperature rises sharply as I follow them in. I keep moving forward cautiously, ready to sprint back to the cellar if I need to. Being caught spying is not going to help my situation. The voices fall quiet and I step forward again, past a broad timber strut and into a large cave-like room. Pa and the Aireys are so engrossed in what they're doing I'm certain they won't notice me.

The space in which I'm standing has been hollowed out of the earth and is supported at intervals with tall wooden struts; some look ancient, but others look like they've only recently been fitted. Piles of rubble lie about as if the cave is prone to sudden rockfalls. I keep my head low and pull my cape up over my head, as if that will offer any protection.

Pa and the Aireys are busy with an assortment of long-handled tools that had been left leaning against the far wall. Pa's holding something that looks like a hoe but which has been sharpened at the end. One of the Aireys is busy examining something that looks like a long metal spear, and the other is using a large file to sharpen a long-handled spade.

I take hesitant steps forward. In the middle of the cave is a small scaffold that reaches up to the roof. I watch in amazement as Pa leaps up it with ease; I don't think I've ever seen him so nimble. The three have stopped talking to each other, as if this is a well-rehearsed routine. One of the Aireys passes all the tools up to him and Pa places them on the wide floorboards at the top of the scaffold. Eventually, huffing and wheezing, the Aireys haul themselves up the scaffold and join Pa at the top.

It's only at this point that I think to look up. Above the scaffold is a sight that doesn't make any sense at all. The entire roof area of the cave is made up of a low-slung, bulging, rubbery material. It's as if the ceiling is sagging! But it's more than that. The ceiling is heaving up and down, and trembling slightly. Small, round metal plates cover its entire surface.

I'm aware my mouth is hanging open, so close it quickly and watch in horror as Pa begins to prod at whatever is above him with his hoe. Swearing loudly he keeps prodding until eventually his hoe breaks through the rubbery surface. A distant wail comes from somewhere else in the house and red liquid seeps out of the newly cut area and drips on to Pa's head. Is it possible it's blood? I clasp a hand over my mouth in horror. What is Pa doing? And what is he doing it to?

"Be quick, man, or that damned Druid will be on the rampage," hisses one of the Aireys.

"Well, I'll be quicker if you come and help," Pa snaps.

The two Aireys reach up and between them they manage to wedge their implements beneath one of the metal plates. Once it has been loosened, Pa stretches up, jiggles it about, and eventually it breaks free. Another distant wail causes my heart to pound in anguish. More red liquid trickles from the wound. The distinct smell of iron fills the room. Whatever is above our heads is bleeding.

"Let's get out now in case it starts thrashing around," Pa says, leaping down from the scaffolding and tossing his hoe towards the corner of the room.

It's time to leave. I hoist my skirts up and race the length of the tunnel, back into the cellar where I quickly grab an armful of feathers and run at full pelt through the cellar rooms, up the stone flight of stairs, along the corridor, through the kitchens, past Mrs Edwards, who is too absorbed in the task of filleting a giant fish to notice me, and out into the yard.

Whatever Pa says about my overactive imagination, I know I didn't imagine that. I head for the workshop and Medwyn, wondering whether I can possibly tell him about what I just saw.

Chapter Ten

I burst into the workshop. Medwyn looks at me as if he's just seen a ghost.

"Are you all right?" he says, as I toss the feathers into a pile in the corner of the room.

"Yes, yes, I'm fine," I say, aware my hands are still trembling. He'll think I've lost my mind if tell him what just happened. He doesn't think much of Pa as it is and he'll think even less of him if I tell him what I saw.

"I just didn't have much success, that's all. The dresses were so ancient they fell apart in my hands. It was like they were made of tissue. But the feathers look perfect!" I pick one up and hold it up to the light.

"You don't look fine," he says, not remotely interested in the feather.

I stare at my boots.

"Did something happen in the cellar?"

I desperately want to trust him, but I'm still not sure.

"No," I say quietly, looking away.

He takes a deep breath, as if he too is weighing up what to say. "Did you see more than feathers and old dresses down there?" He picks up another feather and smooths its ruffled vanes. I wonder if he's ever been tempted to go down there. He comes to our house every day to stoke and feed the furnace. Has he ever wondered what lies beneath it?

"Oh no," I say. "Nothing of interest, apart from the crumbled remains of my family's past. But for now I need to think about where to get the fabric we need. We'll never build a flying machine if we don't have anything to cover the wings."

"There's that fabric shop in Menai Bridge," Medwyn says, still eying me suspiciously, "but it'll cost a fortune from there."

A little idea begins to worm its way around my brain. Aunty Efa has a lot of dresses. Far more than she needs. There are only seven days in the week, after all, and she must have at least twenty. And it seems she's been accepting money from Pa to turn a blind eye to whatever he's up to. So would it be that bad if I borrowed a couple?

"Leave it with me," I say.

I dart out of the workshop and run back into the house, certain Aunty Efa is out for the day. I race up the stairs and along the corridor towards her room, my mind alive with worry about what Pa's up to. However impossible it sounds, I'm certain whatever he was prodding with his hoe was alive – even though that doesn't make any sense at all. And it's trapped and at the mercy of Pa and the Aireys. I decide to go down and take another look when no one's around.

I reach the door to Aunty Efa's room and knock quietly, glancing each way along the corridor. The house is silent. I slowly turn the door handle, holding my breath as it opens with a loud creak. I step into the room and close the door behind me. Aunty Efa's red and gold velvet curtains are open and hooked back on huge, gilt holdbacks. It's gloomy outside, and with her red flock wallpaper and dark four-poster bed the room feels dingy and oppressive.

Dozens of lifeless mannequin eyes watch me coolly as I stand and scan the room, my heart pounding with the shame of what I'm about to do. Some of the mannequins are little more than headless torsos – functional items designed to carry a gown, but the ones that have heads and limbs have an almost human quality, and I shudder as I walk past each of them, shrinking under their silent gaze. I wish I'd listened more when Aunty Efa went on about her dresses and what fabric they were made from. Words such as *silk, chiffon, satin, taffeta* and *moire* leap into my mind, but I've no idea which is which. Le Bris said in his letter a strong fabric was "vital to the integrity of the wing", one that could withstand the force of the wind rushing across it. I approach each mannequin in turn and touch the fabric of each dress. Many of them are heavily made up, and without thinking what I'm doing I reach up to touch the sculpted wax cheek of one whose dress I'm examining. The cheek is red and sticky, suggesting Aunty Efa has recently applied rouge to it.

Fearful of her returning home unexpectedly, I go from dress to dress, tugging at the fabric, rubbing it between my fingers, holding it up to the light. I eventually decide on four dresses that seem to be made from the thickest and most robust fabric. The skirts are all huge, protruding several feet from the waist, so I'm sure they'll supply the quantity I need.

I quickly pull the dresses off the mannequins and toss them into a pile by the door before hiding the now-naked mannequins in a corner of the room, so it's not immediately obvious that someone has been in here. It's entirely possible Aunty Efa won't even notice at all! When I'm sure I've left everything as tidy as possible, I scoop up the armful of gowns and head back to the workshop.

Chapter Eleven

Medwyn has gone when I get back. I drop the dresses on to the floor, relieved to let go of them; they're so heavy, they must be horrible for Aunty Efa to wear. I'm just kicking them into a pile next to the feathers when a clattering of hooves and wheels in the yard breaks the silence. I poke my head out of the workshop door just in time to see a fast cob and a small cart tearing into the yard. The driver calls out a command and they come to a sudden stop just feet from the workshop door. The driver throws her hood back; it's Aunty Dilys, with Medwyn by her side. He climbs down unsteadily, his normally red cheeks chalk white.

"Sorry about that," he says, emerging through a cloud of dust. "She's in a bit of a hurry."

Aunty Dilys jumps down from the cart and strides towards me, her mouth set in a thin line. For a moment I think she's going to tell me off about something, and I shrink away from her, but before I know what's happening she pulls me into an embrace, wrapping me tightly in her arms. I try to wriggle free, but she's far too strong.

"Oh, you poor, poor girl," she says, pulling me in tighter, pressing my cheek into one of her armpits.

I can't remember the last time anyone held me like this. Pa's not the hugging type, and neither is Aunty Efa. Feeling my eyes begin to swell, I blink my tears away and allow myself to go limp in her arms. Struggling slightly to draw breath, I stare down at her leather spats, inhaling her scent of sea and woodsmoke. She eventually releases me and holds me at arm's length. I look up at her shyly. She has one of those weathered faces you see on people who live their lives outside, and the kindest of eyes.

"Now, you mustn't worry about a thing," she says.

"I've talked to Jones the Coracle and everything is sorted."

"Um, w-what do you mean?" I stammer.

She nods towards her cart. Dozens of wooden batons are protruding from the back of it, all held together in an old dust sheet.

"Is that the wood for the wings?" I whisper, looking from her to Medwyn and then back at the cart.

She nods. "Medwyn has explained everything."

"It's what Mr Jones uses for his coracles," Medwyn says. "I think it'll be perfect."

"It will!" I say, running to the cart, touching the slim struts as if they're the most precious things in the world. "But surely we need to pay him for it?"

"Nope. Not a sausage," Aunty Dilys says. "He owes me a favour."

I hug her again. "Thank you," I whisper.

She glances up at the house, squinting. "And does your pa know about your little project?"

"Sort of," I say, crossing my fingers behind my back, "but he doesn't think I'll be able to do it."

"Well, what does he know about building giant artificial birds?" she says.

"It will work!" I say, suddenly realising she's just humouring me. "The Frenchman proved it works!"

"Whatever you say," she says, "and if you don't happen to fly like a bird, you can always have a nice ride along the sands."

"It will work," I repeat. "I'm going to fly, Aunty Dilys!"

She rolls her eyes, but doesn't say any more on the subject.

"Let's unload the wood," Medwyn says, pulling the dust sheet away and passing it to his aunt. He starts to carry the long batons into the workshop.

"Come on, get cracking, you two," Aunty Dilys says, folding up the sheet and tossing it into the cart. "I need to get out before the tide comes back in."

"Are you going out on the water?" I say, feeling the sudden draw of the sea, wondering when I'll be able to take my coracle out again.

"No, she's off worm picking," Medwyn says, smiling at his aunt. They seem to like each other so much, I can't help feeling a twinge of envy.

"Ah," I say. "Well, I hope you fill all your buckets!"

She nods to me, leaps up into her cart, cracks her whip and sets off down the drive in a cloud of dust.

"It's perfect," I say as we stack the lengths of timber in the workshop. "I think we have most of the parts we need now." I point to the pile of stolen gowns. "I even have the fabric."

Medwyn crouches down next to the dresses and examines one. "I'm worried about what your Aunty Efa will do when she finds out, Wren. You don't want her trying to stop you doing this."

"She won't notice. She's got more than she needs anyway." I don't mention how I think she's been funding her dress-buying. I'm not going to feel guilty about this.

"And you're really happy to use your coracle?" he says. "We could try to build something. There might be enough spare wood to make a hull."

"It'll be easier than building something from scratch, and, look, according to Le Bris, the safest way to land is on the water, so a boat's the perfect thing. And we can always take the wings off when I want it back as a coracle again."

Medwyn picks up one of the dresses and holds the fabric up to the light. "It's going to look like the strangest bird!" he says.

"But if it flies, who cares?"

We sit down to discuss the best way to approach the build. Ma always talked me through what she was doing, and I decide we need to take the same step-by-step approach. My heart is thundering with excitement, but still there's an annoying sensible voice at the back of my mind telling me there's no way on earth I'm going to be able to make this pile of random items lift up into the air and fly.

Chapter Twelve

Building a flying machine takes much longer than I expected. I'd imagined simply lashing all the parts together, but, as Ma always said, nothing worth doing in life is ever straightforward. Pa hasn't mentioned the institution for a few days, but I still don't trust him to have changed his mind. I have two weeks before the date of my incarceration, and if I don't get my flying machine finished, I'll have to think about another means of escape. I've been thinking a lot about what's going on underneath the house too, but haven't had a chance to go again on my own. Pa is always attached to the bunch of keys. They're always visible as a knobbly lump in his trouser pocket, but I'm biding my time, waiting for the right moment.

Every time I meet Medwyn in the workshop I feel a rush of excitement at the sight of our machine taking shape, and the thought that very soon I might fly through the sky like a bird. Using Monsieur Le Bris's plans, we build a wooden framework for each wing, taking care to ensure the shape is just right. We glue each piece together, securing every joint with wire. It only takes two days to make the frames for the wings and the tail using Aunty Dilys's batons. When we're done, I hold one of the wings up. It's enormous!

"What's the word the Frenchman used," Medwyn says, examining our handiwork, "to describe how the shape of it helps it lift into the air?"

"Aspiration," I say. "If you get the shape exactly right, the wind will travel over the top and the bottom of it at different rates, and that's what will lift you up into the air."

He nods. "And have you thought about who you'll ask to tow you?"

I've been thinking about this a lot. Le Bris said he used a fast horse and cart to tow him. As soon as he lifted up, he untied the rope that was attached to the cart. He said you have to get the speed just right, but the basic principle was, the faster the better.

I hear a horn tooting and the rumble of wheels in the distance. It seems to be coming from the gardens. Medwyn and I look at each other.

"It's worth asking," he says. "You never know."

"I'll catch her when she's in a good mood," I say, wondering how I can possibly persuade her to tow me up into the sky after what happened with Ma and her. But you never know. She still hasn't said a thing about the dresses so I wonder if she's even noticed some of them are missing. She was a bit off with me the night after I stole them, but since then has been back to her normal self, talking to anyone who'll listen about fashion, feathers and finery, or arguing with Pa. "And I was thinking, we'll need a long stretch of flat ground. We could do it when the tide's out, Medwyn. The inlet at the side of the church might be long enough. The wet sand will be a bit soft, but I'm sure it'll do."

"And then you'll need to land on the water."

I nod.

"But not near the Swellies!"

"If I do, that'll be the last time you see me!"

I look at my coracle with longing, wondering if I'll ever get it back on the water. But this is a worthy sacrifice. I'll just have to pray it survives the force of my landing when the time comes.

Medwyn picks up one of the feathers from the pile and smooths it out, blowing on it until it fluffs up. "A bird made a big sacrifice to let us have this. The least we can do is look after it." He places all the feathers, shafts first, into an empty box. "This should keep them safe until we need them," he says.

They do look splendid in their various shades of red. "It'll look like it's on fire, when they're all attached," I whisper.

"Like a phoenix," he says.

I grin at him, imagining myself swooping through the sky, like a giant, flaming phoenix.

"To the Phoenix!" I say, raising an imaginary glass to Medwyn.

"To the Phoenix," he replies, as we clink fists.

Chapter Thirteen

We eat early tonight as Pa has organised an after-dinner performance with his singing group. He barely talks during dinner, and doesn't make any fuss at all when Aunty Efa arrives late. He smelled of wine before he'd even had a drink at the table and seems to have lost all control of his forehead worm. I wonder if his dishevelled state is anything to do with what's going on underneath the house, or because of me. I want to ask him about what I saw in the cellar, but then I'd have to confess to being down there in the first place. And he'd probably lie anyway. I keep my head down. I don't even want to look at him.

The table is cleared swiftly after dinner, moved to the side of the room, and the chairs laid out in rows. Everyone, including Mrs Edwards, the cook, who barely ever leaves the kitchen, comes in to join us. Pa and his singers are to be accompanied by a harpist tonight. Somehow he's got Nerys Evans from Bangor, one of the best harpists in North Wales, to come to our house. He scuttles about, being bossy and snappy with everyone, telling everyone where to stand as they come in, getting Nerys to move her giant harp to the left, and then back to where it started, and generally fussing about and annoying everyone.

"Come on, come on! We don't have all day," he snaps, beckoning in a late arrival.

The harpist begins and everyone falls silent. Her hands glide, ghost-like, over the strings, creating a sound that makes the hairs on the back of my neck stand on end. It's as if she and the harp are one.

After her introduction, the group, a mixture of men and women, begin to sing. I recognise some of them from that evening in the church. They're all dressed in their Sunday best, the men in dark suits with stiff collars, the women in long black dresses.

They begin quietly, allowing the harp to take the lead. They're singing a strange choral version of *"Hela'r Dryw"*, or "Hunting the Wren". It isn't my favourite song for obvious reasons, and I can't help wondering why Pa has chosen to perform it tonight.

The women's voices pierce the air like crystal, with the male voices providing a deep bass undertone. Pa seems a million miles away, as if the song is a balm to his troubled mind. He swings his hips gently from side to side, his eyes closed. They eventually finish to a polite round of applause. Pa opens his eyes, presses his hands together and bows, and the others follow his lead.

"And now we'd like to perform a special song," he says, "which I'd like to dedicate to my daughter." He stares at me pointedly.

My heart sinks. He made a promise years ago never to sing his "special song" ever again. He presses his fingers to his lips and nods to the harpist, who lifts her hands and begins to play.

They start in the usual way, singing familiar verses written centuries ago by a nameless bard. I pull a face at Pa, but he seems oblivious to any of us, enunciating the words in his rich voice that reverberates around the room, almost entirely obscuring the harp's gentler tones. The singers alternate between Welsh and English for each verse, singing words of praise for the heroic endeavours of Gruffudd ap Bleddyn ap Llewelyn, the one with the chin like mine.

The song is entirely directed at me. The mortification I felt in the church returns, setting my cheeks on fire. I fix my eyes on my lap, trying to force my ears not to hear, but I can't cut out the voices filling the room. I don't think I've ever properly listened to this song before, but now the words thrust their way towards me, knocking at my consciousness, demanding to be let in. Words repeated over and over. *Captive. Bravery. Struggle. Soar.* My mind is like one of the whirlpools in the Swellies. Images of Pa in the cellar, the Aireys, the song from the roof, the thing beneath the house, my impending imprisonment, all tumble around as I try to make sense of what's going on. Something's happening around us, and no one wants to talk about it. I feel a sudden rage towards Pa and his ridiculous song and continue to stare at my lap in silent rebellion.

The singing eventually stops. Pa bows to us, spins to face his fellow singers and bows to them. "Thank you for a rapturous performance, as always," he says. Despite the thread veins scattered about his cheeks, he's deathly pale.

Everyone eventually leaves in a flurry of chatter and clicking heels, and Pa starts stacking the sheet music into a tidy pile. I approach him, my heart thudding. "You said you were never going to sing that song again," I say quietly.

"Oh, don't be ridiculous. I thought we hadn't sung it for a while, that's all. And it's good to remember the man. We wouldn't want his deeds forgotten. You of all people should know that."

"Me of all people?" I hiss. "What does that mean? And what does the song mean? It doesn't even make any sense!"

Pa looks at me, his face reddening. "This is exactly your problem, Wren! Your blind refusal to accept who and what you are. You make no effort whatsoever to embrace your responsibilities."

His face is now inches from mine, but I stare back at him, determined for once to hold his gaze.

"This is why I'm having to take desperate measures." He narrows his eyes at me and drops his voice a notch. "It's because of you," he drawls, "that we are in this situation."

"Because of me?" I shout. "And what situation are we in? What are you talking about, Pa?"

"Oh, you know what I mean. If you were ever in a position of choosing between the family and all this –" he waves a hand around the room – "and your blasted principles – rescuing things and messing about on the water like some sort of seabird – then I very much suspect you'd be tempted to make the wrong choice."

"You're not making any sense, Pa!" I shout. "I have no idea what you're talking about!" I glare up at him, my hands on my hips, wishing I wasn't so small.

"It seems you've quite lost your mind, Wigbert," Aunty Efa says, steaming up to us. "We're living in the nineteenth century, not the thirteenth. What with the skull incident and now this. You're getting embarrassing. People are starting to talk. Why don't you sing about the mountains? Or the birds? Or anything else really. Just not that man."

Pa stares at her through glassy eyes. "We have been rehearsing this piece for some time," he says. "I thought you'd enjoy it. And anyway, who are *you* to tell me what to do?"

"I am your wife's sister and I have the misfortune of living with you and your horrid little secrets," she says darkly.

"Well, I'm sorry you find it such a hardship," Pa says.

"What secrets?" I whisper, looking up at him.

111

"Oh, it's nothing," Aunty Efa says, before spinning round and storming out of the room in a cloud of smoke and steam, leaving Pa and me standing glaring at each other.

Pa opens his mouth to say something, but the room suddenly shakes so violently we're forced to grip each other to stay upright.

"Good God, what was that?" he says.

And then the cry comes, louder and clearer than I've ever heard it before.

"Did you hear that?" I whisper. "I told you I hadn't made it up! The noise from the top of the tower! Didn't you just hear it? It sounds like someone's up there. And it sounds like they're singing."

"I think your imagination is getting the better of you again," Pa says, appearing to pull himself together. "It's just the wind being peculiar."

"The wind being peculiar? What are you talking about?" I shout. "You cannot pretend *that* didn't just happen. And what about the room shaking? You can't deny that either!"

"Well, I will concede there may have been a small movement, but it's probably just the house settling for the night." His eyes slide away from me.

"It isn't a dog," I say. "It's a house. Houses don't settle

for the night."

"This is exactly why you need to be somewhere else for a while, until you can learn to listen to sense and reason, rather than indulge your rather colourful imagination!"

I stare at him open-mouthed.

Tudur sidles up to Pa. "It was hardly anything," he says, smirking at me. "I barely felt it at all, Pa."

I glare at him and ball my fists.

"We have got some new cracks, though," he adds. "There's a fresh one in the scullery. It's only little but Mrs Edwards was complaining about the draught coming through it. Says it's like an ice house in there."

"I am indeed aware of that crack," Pa says, "and I have someone coming over in the morning to take a look. It's just part of living in an ancient house, I'm afraid."

I can't help noticing how his tone is very different when he talks to Tudur, and I seethe inside.

We fall into a painful silence, the only noise the ticking of the grandfather clock in the hall. The fire hisses in the grate. The flames on the candles flutter in a light breeze that's appeared from somewhere, bringing with it the smell of the sea. Pa chews on his bottom lip, muttering to himself.

In this moment of silence the house produces another

peculiar noise – a deep groan, like an animal in a trap.

A sudden blast of cold air extinguishes the candles and we're plunged into darkness. We stand like statues, eyes all fixed on the same thing.

A vast crack has appeared at the front of the dining room, running from the floor all the way up to the vaulted ceiling, through which we can see the waves of the strait and the moonlit sky above.

Chapter Fourteen

Pa is examining our latest crack with the builder when I come down for breakfast. Assuming it wouldn't have miraculously healed itself in the night, I've wrapped myself up in a cloak and thick, woollen gloves. Aunty Efa is in a huge fur hat, a blanket wrapped round her shoulders and another spread across her knees. Tudur is in so many layers he looks more like a giant sausage roll than a boy. I wolf breakfast down and run out of the front door before Pa can stop me. It's bitterly cold but the sky is reassuringly blue. The mountains have been coated in fresh snow overnight, and even our little beach has been sprinkled with a thin layer of frost. I'm missing my coracle. Days like this, when the sea is gleaming and the seabirds are skimming the waves, are the best ones to be out on the water. I pray it'll still be seaworthy after my flight.

I light the fire as soon as I reach the workshop and rub my hands together over the small flame.

I've been thinking about what Pa said last night. What did he mean when he talked about me choosing between the house and my principles? But soon I'm fizzing with excitement about the thought of finishing the wings, and push Pa's performance, the peculiar thing under the house, the institution and the new crack in the dining room to the back of my mind.

Today we're planning to start covering the wings with the dress fabric. I find a gluey-looking substance in one of Ma's cupboards; I hope it will be strong enough to hold the fabric in place. With the addition of some strategically placed staples it should be.

I pick up one of the gowns and start to hack at it with a pair of scissors, ignoring the stab of guilt I feel at destroying something so fine. Separating the skirt from

116

the bodice proves to be the most challenging part of the job, and I'm just grinding my boots into the whalebone corset, tearing at the skirt fabric, when Medwyn arrives.

"Remind me never to get on the wrong side of you," he says.

"I shall tear you to pieces!"

"Do you need a hand?" he says, laughing, coming to join me. I can't help grinning at him. Together we tug at the fabric until eventually it separates from the bodice. I stretch it out across the floor to have a good look at it. There must be about six yards of material here; I'm not surprised it weighed so much. I think my clothes are impractical, but this is far worse.

We spend the rest of the morning destroying dresses, extracting slim whalebones from corsets, and removing hundreds of beads and crystals from the bodices. We toss these into an old tin can for future use. I try not to feel too guilty.

Eventually we begin the process of covering the wings. Using a small brush, we spread glue all over the wooden frames and then press the fabric into the glue. The wings don't look *that* birdlike, but all the different dresses we've used create an appealing patchwork appearance.

When we're done, we lean them up against the wall and stand back to admire our handiwork.

"What do you think?" I say.

"I think we've created something truly magnificent!" Medwyn runs a hand along the fabric, gently tapping it to test its strength. He examines every seam and staple to check they're all secure.

I look at him surreptitiously, desperate to talk to him about what's going on in the house, but worry that if he knows Pa's involved in some sort of shady activity, it will drive him away all over again. I'm certain he doesn't like him, or Aunty Efa for that matter.

I start tidying up the workshop and we work together in silence for a while. I can't help noticing him glancing at me from time to time, opening his mouth and closing it again, as if he wants to say something too. At one point he actually says my name, then pretends to forget what it was he wanted to say.

"What is it?" I say. "Spit it out."

I don't think I've seen him look so awkward.

"Well, it's not really my place to say," he says after a moment, "but there's a bit of talk, more general concern really, around these parts, in Menai Bridge, that is, about your pa."

"What sort of talk?" I ask quietly.

"Well, nothing malicious or anything like that. More concern, it is." He falls silent.

"So what are people saying?"

"Well, it's just that Aunty Dilys's cousin was in your house last night."

He sees the look on my face.

"No, it's nothing like that! She wasn't spying. She's in your pa's singing group. She said it was all a bit strange, that's all. That your pa seemed somewhere else in his head, and that he made them sing the song you hate, and that you looked upset. But she said it was more than that. She said your pa was acting strangely, even by his standards."

I ignore the knot in my belly as I decide what to say. "I've got no idea what's going on in Pa's head," I mumble eventually. I wouldn't even know where to start as none of it makes any sense, even to me.

"I was just wondering, I was over in the night, you see, and I couldn't help noticing what's been happening with your house."

"You mean the cracks?"

He nods.

"But why do you come over in the night, Medwyn?" I say, keen to change the subject. "Couldn't someone who works here tend to the furnace if it has to be done then?"

"I wouldn't trust anyone else to do it."

"But why does it have to be you? Haven't you got

enough to do already?"

"It's a bit of a specialist job, see. My pa did it before me, and my grandfather before him, and so on."

"But someone must tell you to come."

"It's just what I've done since Pa died. And if I ever have a child, then they'll do the same, if they're still needed, that is."

"Well, that doesn't sound very fair. What if they don't want to?"

"Oh, they will."

I scoop up a handful of wood and fabric offcuts and toss them into the brazier.

"And is someone coming to repair the cracks?" he asks.

"Pa's got Mr Evans, the builder, round to look at them. I think he's going to try to patch them up."

"But won't they just crop up elsewhere? Shouldn't he be getting to the root cause of the problem?" Medwyn still has that look on his face. The look that suggests he wants to tell me something but can't. Or won't.

"I guess so," I say. I still haven't told anyone what I saw below the house, partly because it doesn't make any sense, and partly because I worry Pa's in terrible trouble, and if there is a living thing down there, then *that's* in even more trouble than Pa. And now with Medwyn talking about our cracks, I'm suddenly wondering if the two things might even be linked. I'll have to work out how to separate Pa from his keys and get back down to the cellar. There's no way he's going to tell me what's going on. I'll just have to find out for myself.

I wonder if Emrys might know something. Realising I haven't seen him for a while, I decide to go and talk to him and check he's safe.

Chapter Fifteen

I reach the ice house and knock on the door. Hearing no reply, I turn the handle, push the door open and step into the small, low-ceilinged lobby, closing the door quietly behind me. I take tentative steps across the uneven brick floor.

I whisper Emrys's name as I walk further into the gloom but am met with silence. Could the Aireys really have carried out their threat?

I reach the narrow door that leads to the subterranean storage area, open it cautiously and find myself on a narrow ledge that encircles a vast, egg-shaped hollow, once the main ice chamber. The drop into it must be more than twenty feet. I keep my body pressed against the wall and call out again. I shuffle crab-like round the ledge until I reach the wooden ladder that leads down to the bottom of the pit. Like the lobby, the whole place is lined with bricks. Taking a deep breath, I climb down the ladder and jump into the bottom of the bowl. I can't imagine what it must have been like when it was full of ice and how cold it must have been down here. But when I touch the floor I'm surprised to find it warm.

I spot a low door on the opposite side of the space and take a small hesitant step towards it, but freeze when it swings open with a loud creak.

A small, hooded figure emerges, carrying a small bowl.

I hold my breath, my heart pounding.

The person throws their hood back. It's Emrys. Of course it's Emrys! I'm just feeling jumpy with everything going on.

"Emrys!" I say, overwhelmed by relief. "Are you all right?" I hold my candle up to get a better look at him.

He looks at me through pale, watery eyes. "Ah, young Wren of the house," he says. "What in the name of goodness are you doing down here?" He places the bowl on the floor to the side of the door.

"I just came to see how you were," I say, trying to sound bright, attempting to identify an unusual medicinal smell now filling the room. "I thought I hadn't seen you for a while."

He narrows his eyes suspiciously. "I believe you might have seen me just the other day. I seem to remember discussing Mrs Edwards's duck."

"Ah yes," I say, "but I just wanted to check all was well, and I can see it is, so I'll leave you alone."

A shadow flickers across his face. It might just be the flame from my candle, but I'm certain he looks worried.

I glance at the door behind him, wondering where it leads to. Noticing me looking, he closes it quietly with a sandalled foot.

We face each other for a moment, him shuffling from one foot to the other, and me hot and red-faced, feeling as if I've been caught trespassing.

"I'm about to begin my morning exercises," he says. "You are, of course, welcome to join me."

He steps on light feet towards a roll of bedding at the other side of the bowl. I've seen the contortions he sometimes twists his body into and the idea of attempting such a thing is distinctly unappealing. "Thank you," I say. "I'd love to normally, but I have some jobs to do, for Pa." I glance at the door he just came through. "Does that lead anywhere?" I say, trying to sound like I'm not too interested.

"Oh, no, no, no," he says. "Just to a small tunnel." He claps a hand to his mouth. "Oh, oh, what am I saying? I'm so befuddled these days! It just leads to a little storeroom." He shakes his head as if cross with himself.

I know he's lying, but why does he need to lie to me? I'm not Pa!

"So it doesn't lead anywhere if it's just a storeroom?"

"Oh, no, no, no," he says again, lowering himself to a cross-legged position.

"So do you know of any rooms, or anything else, underneath our house? I think there's something strange going on, Emrys, and I'm trying to work out what it is." I don't add that I'm worried about him and what the Aireys might do if they find him.

Emrys closes his eyes, lowers his head and holds his hands together as if in prayer. "Oh, young Wren, it is a terrible thing to be so shackled when all you wish for is to soar up into the clouds, as free and high as a bird."

"Do you know what I've been building?" I say. "Did Medwyn tell you?" I suddenly want to tell him all about my project, and my dream of flying up into the sky and far away, far away from Pa and the Aireys and their horrible institution, and even far from Aunty Efa and Tudur too. Free to be me. Just Wren. Not some memory of a long-dead chieftain.

He opens his eyes and looks up at me. "My dear, if you have been building something, that is news to me." And with that he bends forward, places his hands on the floor and lifts his slim body up into the air, his long lean legs stretching up towards the roof of the ice house.

He seems to have decided our conversation is over, and I creep out with even more questions swirling about my mind and a determination to see what lies through that little door.

Chapter Sixteen

When I get to the workshop, still mulling over Emrys's words about flying away, I find Medwyn gluing feathers to one of the wings.

"I think you were right about these," he says.

"It's going to look magnificent!" I whisper, unable to draw my eyes away from the giant wing he's working on. I think Ma would have approved. She'd probably have said the feathers were *unnecessary fripperies*, but deep down she'd have liked it.

Medwyn hands me the pot of glue and puts the kettle on the brazier. "I'll make us a hot cordial to celebrate our achievement."

"We're nearly there, Medwyn!" I say. "We just have to attach the wings to the coracle and it'll be done." I look over the pile of parts, not quite believing my own words.

"Just…?" Medwyn says, pulling a face.

Ma would have planned this part of the build before she'd even begun, but I'm sure we'll work it out. I dip the brush into the pot of glue and begin the laborious process of attaching each feather one by one. I've no idea if they'll fall off once I'm airborne, but who cares? If they do, they'll just float to the ground, like a shower of embers.

Medwyn looks at me pointedly. "Aunty Dilys says the weather should be nice tomorrow, with a gentle breeze. It might be the perfect weather for flying!"

"How does she know what the weather's going to be doing?" I ask.

"She read it in the worms. They stay nice and deep when it's going to be bad, and come up to the surface when they're expecting it to be fine. She says they're quite reliable in that regard."

I don't know if he's making it up, but I like the idea

of worms predicting the weather, so I don't argue. "And you think we might be ready by then?" Until now this has been a theoretical dream, so the idea of actually trying to fly suddenly grips me with fear.

He looks at me and raises both eyebrows. "If we get on with it, it might."

For a moment I worry what Pa will say when he finds out his only daughter is planning to do the very thing that killed her ma. I force the feeling away. This is nothing to do with him. He does exactly as he pleases, so why shouldn't I?

"I've been reading through the letter again," Medwyn says. "I don't think Le Bris managed to fly for more than a few minutes. Have you thought how long you might be able to stay up?"

I haven't thought about much else. Part of me wants to soar up into the air, fly high above the water and head to the mountains, never to be seen again. But I need to see if this works first before I get ahead of myself. I suspect I won't get that far, at least on my first flight. "Our design will be better than his," I say, trying to sound confident. "And also, I think it depends on what the air's doing. He mentioned an invisible force in the sky, the movement of air that allows birds to soar and to stay aloft without flapping their wings, so I guess it will

129

all depend on that." I don't really understand everything Le Bris said, but am hoping it will become clear when I'm up there. It's always difficult to imagine something you've never experienced. I try not to think about all the things that could go wrong. I might not even get up into the air or, worse still, the Phoenix might just fall apart at the seams, and I'll tumble, in a tangle of feathers, coracle and silk dresses, into the sea.

"Have you asked your aunt yet," Medwyn says, "if she'll tow you?"

"Not exactly," I say, meaning I haven't dared to broach the subject at all. I can't believe she'll help, but perhaps some of her inner daredevil remains, buried deep inside. "I've just got to wait for the right moment."

We spend the rest of the morning working on the tail of the Phoenix, designing and building the controls to make it go up and down, and left to right. Like everything else, it's far more complicated than I thought it would be. We find a roll of cord in one of Ma's drawers and decide it should be suitable for controlling the tail. It's a bit thin and worn in parts, but I'm sure it'll be strong enough. Within just a few hours we have created a complicated web of cord that weaves round a series of brass pulleys inside the coracle's hull. I climb into it to make sure there's still room for me to sit inside. I pull each length of cord in turn, noting how the tail moves with each tug. This simple arrangement of cord is the thing I'll rely on most when I'm up in the sky.

Chapter Seventeen

Mr Thomas is coming in after lunch for an afternoon of misery with Tudur and me in the justice room. I daren't miss lessons, as the last time I tried Pa was so furious I thought his forehead worm was going to explode. I don't want to give him an excuse to ship me off even earlier than planned. I need to keep my head down.

When I get to the justice room, I find not only Tudur

and Mr Thomas waiting for me, but Pa and Aunty Efa too. The room is smoky, and not just from the wheelchair. The fireplace is belching out plumes of reddish-grey smoke. A tendril drifts towards me and snakes its way up to my nostrils. It smells acrid, like Tudur's bedroom first thing in the morning. I clamp my hands over my mouth.

"What's wrong with the fire?" I say through my fingers.

"If I knew that, I'd have resolved the problem," Pa snaps.

I sit down at my desk next to Tudur and he smirks at me in the way he always does if he thinks I'm in trouble. I snarl at him.

Lessons aren't normally held in here, but apparently there's a problem with Pa's study that he doesn't want to talk about. Despite this room's dark history of my family condemning people to imprisonment in Beaumaris Gaol or worse, it was Ma's study when she was alive and there are still memories of her on the walls and the shelves. Pa has been slowly making the room his own, deciding a while ago it would be useful storage for his fishing gear. The walls are now lined with fishing rods of varying sizes, and the drawers of Ma's desk are stuffed with fishing tackle. But old posters of Ma and Aunty Efa remain on the walls; perhaps Pa couldn't bear to take them down, despite his ongoing embarrassment about who and what Ma was.

Aunty Efa is fiddling with her steam engine and tips a small quantity of coal into her fire, causing a fresh plume of smoke to billow from beneath her wheels and up into the room.

"Do you have to do that right now?" Pa hisses. "Isn't it smoky enough in here already?"

"I need to keep it alight. You know that."

Pa shakes his head and sinks to his knees in front of the fire. He peers up the chimney, vainly attempting to waft away the smoke now engulfing him. In all the commotion I hadn't noticed Mr Thomas standing by the window. He's looking even more annoyed with the situation than Pa, and I suspect more desperate to get out of here than me. He opens a window and the room is instantly filled with a fresh sea breeze, clearing the air sufficiently to reveal my favourite poster of Ma and Aunty Efa on the opposite wall. Ma had it printed when they were about to attempt their first-ever stunt.

INTRODUCING

The Astonishing Daredevil Sisters of Rhosneigr

Dare to watch Bronwen Griffiths fire Efa Griffiths
through the barrel of a cannon across the waters of
the Menai Strait!

Never before has such a feat been attempted!
(And perhaps it never will again!)
11.00 a.m. 8 July 1845
The Griffin Inn, Menai Bridge
(weather-dependent)

I run my fingers along the black-and-white sketch, presumably drawn by Ma or Aunty Efa. Ma looks about fifteen and is dressed in breeches. A much younger and smaller Aunty Efa, dressed in frilly pantaloons and bodice, is standing with her, looking nothing like a daredevil. They're positioned either side of an enormous metal cylindrical device, which I believe Ma built. She has a steely, determined look on her face. Aunty Efa looks terrified. I think she was only about my age at the time. My grandparents had been furious with Ma when they'd found posters advertising the spectacle glued to every noticeboard on Anglesey, and then things had got much worse when Aunty Efa had nearly drowned after landing in deep water on the far side of the strait. She told me later that Ma had forgotten to connect the rubber springs needed to limit the distance she flew. She'd been dragged, half dead, out of the water by a passing fishing boat. Both girls had been declared Wales's youngest daredevils, and Aunty Efa the first Welsh human cannonball. But they'd still been in terrible trouble with their parents.

Smoke continues to billow out of the fireplace. Mr Thomas mutters under his breath. Pa swears. Tudur sits at his desk, his immaculately greased head down, scribbling formulae on to a slate.

Mr Thomas seems to have made a decision. "I'll come back tomorrow," he announces. "These conditions are not suitable for learning."

"We could go to the study," Tudur suggests. "What do you think, Pa?"

I glare at him. What's he thinking? This is the perfect excuse to get out of lessons.

"No one is to go into my study," Pa says through gritted teeth.

Our house is enormous, and we have more rooms than we could ever use, but I'm assuming Pa would deem all of them unsuitable for one reason or another.

And, anyway, I'm not going to suggest an alternative.

"Just go," Pa says irritably, waving him away, as if the situation is Mr Thomas's fault.

Mr Thomas nods and stalks from the room.

Aunty Efa is at Ma's bookshelves. She waves me over. "Would you pass me that one, Wren?" she whispers, pointing at a book up on the top shelf. "While your pa's busy."

I climb up the library step and stand on my tiptoes to try to reach it.

"That's the problem with being called Wren," Tudur says, laughing.

I spin to face him. "What are you talking about?"

"I'm just saying that with a name like Wren, you're never going to be much more than a very small person."

"Oh, shut up, Tudur, you pointless human being," I say, turning away from him and straining to reach the book. I don't know why he does this. And now Pa's looking at me as if *I'm* doing something wrong.

"Pa, I was just thinking you should have called her 'Buzzard', or even 'Osprey'. She might have been a bit bigger then," Tudur says, laughing at his own joke.

Pa looks at him with a slightly perplexed expression on his face. He shakes his head and turns back to the chimney.

Tudur looks crestfallen.

I smirk at him, then I take a little leap and grab for the book, just managing to catch the bottom edge of it allowing it to tumble on to Aunty Efa's lap. A lump rises in my throat. It's Ma's copy of the *Mabinogion*, a collection of Welsh legends written hundreds of years ago – stories of chivalry and love and bravery. Ma wasn't a big reader, but she always read these to me when I was little. The book has fallen open at the beginning of the story of Lludd and Llefelys.

"Thank you," Aunty Efa says quietly, closing the book and slipping it inside her fur muff.

I make a spur-of-the-moment decision, while she seems to be in a friendly mood.

"Aunty Efa," I whisper, leaning in close, "I need your help with something."

"Oh yes, what's that?"

"Well, I think I've sort of built an artificial bird. A flying machine."

She looks at me, her eyes wide.

"It's a different design to the one Ma and you built. And I really think it'll work. I've had advice from someone who knows. Someone who's done it already."

She clasps my arm, and I take this as encouragement to go on.

"And I just need someone to tow me, to help me take off. I was thinking, your wheelchair is pretty fast, and I know it's strong. Do you think you might be able to help me?" My heart is hammering at an alarming rate as the words fall out of my mouth.

"Dear God," she says, clutching a hand to her chest. "Oh, no, no, Wren. What were you thinking?"

My cheeks are starting to burn. "Um, that I wanted to try to fly like Ma, and prove that the two of you weren't stupid to think you could do it." I don't mention that I want to fly away from all this, and from Pa and all his secrets and his horrible plans for me.

"But it's not up to you to prove that! You're a child, Wren! You're just a girl!" she shouts, gripping my arm so hard now I cry out in pain.

Pa gets up from the fireplace and walks towards us, his face ashen. He seems to have aged by about ten years in the last few days.

"What have you done, Wren?" he says slowly, with quiet menace.

"I've just been building a flying machine, that's all, Pa!" I say, trying to make it sound like it's nothing at all.

His face turns a shade of puce. "A flying machine?" he shouts, his face now inches from mine. "Have you totally lost your mind?" He runs a hand through his hair. "You stupid, stupid girl! What were you thinking?"

I bite my lip to stop myself from crying. "I just want to do it, Pa! I want to know what it feels like. And I won't make the same mistakes Ma made!" I regret saying that as soon as the words have left my mouth.

"She didn't make any mistakes, Wren," Aunty Efa says. "It was a ridiculous idea, and we should never have tried. I have learned to accept my limitations, Wren, and you should too!"

"But I have the plans from Monsieur Le Bris," I say. "Someone who's already proved it's possible. He lifted up into the air, Pa, and he flew like an albatross!"

"Oh, this confirms every suspicion I've ever had about you, Wren!" Pa says. "You are totally and absolutely out of control. I've tried to be nice to you. I've really tried. But what more can I do? You don't listen to a word I say, you ignore all my attempts to turn you into an acceptable young lady, you try to do everything your way, without giving two hoots about how it makes everyone else feel."

"You've never been nice to me!" I shout, my heart thundering. "All you ever do is tell me how everything I do is wrong, that it's some sort of crime to go out on the water looking at birds." I square up to him, my eyes filling with tears. "And I do care about how other people feel! I never do anything to hurt anyone else." I glare at him. "Unlike some people."

I think for a moment he's going to hit me. "And what exactly do you mean by that?" he says darkly.

"Nothing," I say, looking away.

He narrows his eyes and takes a deep breath. "Well, that's it," he says. "You've blown it, Wren. I shall send a message to the Aireys requesting an urgent place be made for you at the institution. This has gone too far."

"No, you can't, Pa!" I cry. "It hasn't gone too far at all. I just wanted to build a flying machine, that's all."

"I have enough going on," Pa hisses, "without a daredevil for a daughter threatening to repeat history. I won't have it, Wren, do you understand? I forbid you to take this project any further!" He leans in towards me. "I'll set fire to all of it. I'll burn the whole workshop down if I have to. And you, my dear, are keeping your feet very firmly on the ground."

And with that he storms from the room, and as he does so I'm sure I hear him stifle a sob.

What was I thinking asking Aunty Efa in front of Pa? I'm such a fool. I flee from the room, and only allow my tears to start falling as I reach my bedroom and have slammed my door behind me. I throw myself on to my bed and weep.

Chapter Eighteen

I wake up early after a terrible night's sleep. I climb out of bed, cross my bedroom and look at myself in my mirror. My eyes are bloodshot and puffy and my cheeks are hollow and empty-looking. I'd decided halfway through the night that Ma would want me to do this, so ignoring everything Pa said, I pull on my work clothes and creep out through the house before he tries to lock me in my room. I need to do this sooner than planned if he's going to visit the Aireys. Once I'm up in the sky, no one will be able to touch me, or the Phoenix.

For a moment, in the darkness of the night, I'd wondered if Ma was trying to escape too when she built her flying machine.

The dogs follow me through the house, into the workshop and settle straight down by the brazier. I glance outside and up at the sky. Already it's bright blue with only a few small clouds floating on the horizon. I stamp my feet and rub my hands as I wait for Medwyn to arrive, feeling the call of the mountains.

The crack of a whip and the shout of a deep female voice breaks the silence. I run outside just in time to see a small cart tearing into the yard. It takes a sharp turn and comes to a sudden halt just outside the workshop door, gravel flying in all directions.

It's Medwyn and Aunty Dilys.

He looks ashen. She's grinning.

She leaps down and wraps me in one of her giant hugs. "Ah, there you are. Bright and early. Medwyn said you'd be up!" She holds me to her bosom with strong arms, and I remain squashed and helpless until she eventually releases me.

Medwyn climbs down from the cart and staggers towards me. "Remind me to walk next time, will you?"

"You take care, you two," Aunty Dilys says, punching Medwyn on the arm. "Don't do anything I wouldn't." And with that she strides back to the cart, leaps up into her seat and heads off down the drive in a cloud of dust.

"Are you all right?" Medwyn says, rubbing his arm.

"Not really." I tell him everything that happened yesterday. "So, you see, I'm going to have to do it now. Today, Medwyn, before it's too late! He even threatened to burn the workshop down."

Medwyn looks worried. "But I can't believe he'd do that. It was your ma's favourite place."

I shrug. "He's behaving so strangely at the moment. I wouldn't put anything past him."

"And you're worried he'll try to destroy the Phoenix too?"

"Possibly. I just don't know what he's capable of at the moment." I hesitate briefly. "Do you think Aunty Dilys might help us? I know she's always busy with her worms and Jones the Coracle, but she might."

Medwyn blows out slowly, his breath forming a cloud of steam in front of him. "I'll ask, but she probably won't want to get involved, after what happened with your ma."

"But will you ask her anyway?" I say. "When you go home for lunch? You never know."

He nods. "But I can't promise anything."

It takes most of the morning to attach the wings to the coracle and after that we design a series of slip knots to attach the Phoenix to its undercarriage. I practise releasing the knots at speed over and over again, as I'll have to let the undercarriage go as soon as I lift into the air.

I stand back to look at what we've created.

It is a little eccentric and looks more like one of Aunty Efa's dresses entangled in a giant prehistoric bird than the feat of engineering it is. But still I grin at Medwyn, proud to have built such a remarkable thing.

"It's magnificent!" he says, smiling so broadly I can see all his teeth. He shakes my hand. "Congratulations to the hardest taskmaster on all of Anglesey!"

"And congratulations to you. I couldn't have done it without you!" I say, shaking his hand vigorously.

I look outside. The sky is still blue, with a high layer of cloud and a range of far-off fluffy peaks. The wind is light. The sun is bright but not too dazzling.

"Perfect weather for flying!" I whisper, my heart thudding.

"Just got to find someone to tow you up now!"

"Just!" I say, rolling my eyes.

I find Medwyn standing by Aunty Dilys's cob and cart in the yard when I return from lunch.

I run up to him. "So, did you ask her?" I say, glancing around. "Did she say yes? Where is she?"

"Well, she didn't say yes exactly." He's looking positively sheepish. "It's just she didn't say no either. And she'll be busy with Jones the Coracle all afternoon, so I'm sure she won't miss her cart for a few hours."

"Medwyn! You stole her cart!" This is the first time I've ever known him to do anything remotely dishonest.

"Well, not strictly. More like borrowed it for a while."

The horse snorts and scrapes an impatient hoof on the ground.

"But the thing is," I say, trying not to sound ungrateful, "we'll need to go fast. Really fast. As fast as that thing will go, in fact. Aunty Dilys fast."

Medwyn looks a bit offended. "I can drive it fast," he mutters.

"As fast as Aunty Dilys?"

He nods.

"So we could try it now?"

"We could! If you're ready."

I grin at him, wishing he didn't look so nervous. "Well then, I'm ready!"

He smiles back at me. "And, on the subject of flying, I

have something else for you. It isn't much. Just something useful, what with the sun and everything." He reaches into his knapsack and pulls out a small, brown-paper parcel and hands it to me. I open it.

"I made them," he says.

I pull the strangest object from the paper and glance up at him. He's grinning at me. I turn it over in my hands. It's similar to a pair of spectacles, but the lenses have been made from the bottoms of two dark-green glass bottles, with each bottle base encased in a leather pouch with a slim leather belt holding everything together.

"Protective eyewear," he says. "To keep the sun and the flies out of your eyes if we do manage to make this work."

I grin at him and hold them up to my face, squinting in the direction of the sun. Its glare is definitely reduced. He helps me tie the buckle at the back of my head and I turn to face him.

He bursts out laughing.

"What?"

"You look like a giant fly!"

I go to the window and peer at my reflection. "Giant flyer, more like."

"Well, not quite giant."

I laugh. "I think they're the best thing anyone has ever

given me." I want to hug him, but that would be strange, so I salute him instead, and instantly realise that's even stranger, but I don't care.

"Well, let's go then," Medwyn says. "What are we waiting for?"

We haul open the long concertina doors that stretch the length of the workshop, revealing the Phoenix, our beautiful flying machine, a hotchpotch of assorted items, all wrapped up in fine fabrics and feathers.

We take a wing each and ease the Phoenix out of the workshop and into the yard. Using the rope we found yesterday, we attach it to the back of Aunty Dilys's cart. Medwyn climbs cautiously into the driver's seat, and I clamber up into my beautiful bird, my heart pounding, pushing all thoughts of Pa to the back of my mind.

Medwyn tows me slowly down through the garden towards the strait, my wings and me bouncing up and down, the rows of ostrich feathers fluttering like flames in the breeze. We must look quite the spectacle, but I'm relieved no one's around to see us, as that means there's no one to stop us.

We trundle over the steep bank of rocky ground that leads down to the beach. Medwyn flicks his whip gently and we continue across sticky sand and mounds of seaweed, picking our way between rocky outcrops and past rock pools left behind by the retreating tide. As Medwyn picks up speed, I grip the sides of my coracle to avoid being tossed out. At lunchtime I'd sneaked into Aunty Efa's bedroom and borrowed her long leather jacket and spare driving hat. My bottle spectacles are wrapped round my wrist, ready to pull on when I need them. I hope I should be sufficiently protected from the chill sea air, and the flies.

We start to trot at a steady pace over the expanse of flat, wet sand. Medwyn keeps glancing back at me, as if to check I'm still there. The tide is way out, further out than I've ever seen it, with just a narrow stretch of water flowing along the middle of the strait. It's almost as if Ma has arranged the weather and the tide to align perfectly, just for me.

"Are you watching, Ma?" I whisper. The only response is the rush of the wind and the caw of the gulls wheeling above.

Medwyn turns back and waves.

A large flock of gulls has gathered above him. I wonder if they're the same birds from the church, keeping an eye on things. They shriek and scream above his head for a few minutes before swooping away in a mass of beating wings and squawking beaks.

I wonder how Ma felt when she was about to go flying

for the first time. I wonder if she was as terrified as I am now.

Eventually we arrive at the inlet to the side of St Tysilio's. When we reach the causeway, Medwyn reins in the pony and we come to a stop. I jump out and land with a squelch in the sand. Medwyn leaps down from the cart and helps me manoeuvre the Phoenix until it's dead straight behind the cart, facing the centre of the strait.

"Are you all right?" he says. "You can still change your mind if you want to." He looks more terrified than me.

"I'm ready," I say, gritting my teeth, suddenly feeling a fierce determination that totally overwhelms any feelings of fear.

I climb back into the Phoenix.

My hands are shaking, but I think now from excitement. It takes a while to get settled into the coracle, straighten out the control cords and check they're all correctly positioned in their pulleys. I sit with my knees bent up in front of me. Medwyn checks everything is lashed into place for what feels like the hundredth time.

I pull my dark spectacles over my eyes and do up the buckle at the back. Medwyn leans in and tightens the strap, examining his handiwork. "They suit you! And when you come back down to earth, you'll return with not a fly in either eye!"

"And undazzled by the sun," I add.

"Good luck!" He salutes me. He's smiling but he looks worried.

"I won't crash, Medwyn!"

"Good!" he says. "I've put too much work into it for you to smash it up. Are you ready?"

I nod, not trusting myself to speak.

Medwyn runs back to the cart and jumps up into the driver's seat. He raises his whip, cracks it high above the pony's flank, and we're off. For a few frustrating moments we travel no quicker than a slow trot.

"Faster!" I shout in frustration.

Medwyn cracks the whip again, but the pony is sluggish without Aunty Dilys to drive it. We're too slow. This will never work.

"We have to go faster!" I shout, noticing that the tide is creeping back in. If we don't make it work this time, we'll lose the only stretch of level ground in the area.

Medwyn twists to look back at me. He nods, as if making a decision, but his face is ashen.

"Come on," I shout. "Don't worry about me!"

Medwyn nods, flicks his whip again, calls out a command to the pony and finally we pick up speed. Soon salty air is rushing over my cheeks, sweeping my breath away. It feels like I'm flying already, and I still haven't left the ground.

The Phoenix judders. We pick up more speed. The wings, now catching the wind, tug at the ropes that connect them to my coracle.

A sudden gust sweeps up underneath me and before I realise what's happening my coracle tugs at the undercarriage as if itching to be free of it. I quickly untie the ropes that connect me to the apple crate and Aunty Efa's old wheels and toss them over the edge.

Almost instantly I soar up into the air, just as Le Bris said I would. The flock of gulls returns and forms a cloud of silent white bodies around me, all looking steadfastly ahead.

For just the briefest moment I spot Medwyn far below, a look of horror on his face, his hand clasped to his mouth. He pulls in the reins and brings the pony to a standstill.

I start to panic, and almost forget everything I'm supposed to be doing and all the things I learned from Le Bris's letter.

Calm down, Wren.

Concentrate!

It's her!

She's with me.

I know it.

I take control of myself, starting with my breathing. I breathe in and out slowly, a difficult process with the wind racing past my face, stealing my breath, making my lips flap like a dog on a cart. But somehow I do it, and my mind begins to clear.

I glance over the side. Medwyn and Aunty Dilys's pony and cart are miles below.

I test the network of cords surrounding me, and look back at my tail.

Everything is working as it should.

I am flying!

I am soaring like a bird!

The gulls remain by my side for a while, but soon they tire of my spectacle and swoop away, back down to Medwyn, leaving me alone in the silence of the sky.

But not quite alone, of course.

As I ease the cords through their pulleys with cold fingers, I feel callused hands on mine, guiding them, reassuring me.

Keep an eye on your tail.

Watch your height.

I nod, so she knows I've heard her, and that I'm listening.

I begin to test my controls; work out what I can and

can't do, how the Phoenix responds to my commands. I pull on each cord, following my well-practised routine, moving the tail up and down and from left to right.

After a while, as my confidence builds, I turn round and head along the strait, soaring high over the towers of the bridge and on towards Beaumaris.

After a few minutes, I take a tight turn and head back over the bridge. My house comes into view and I soar above it. Emrys is in the garden, waving his stick in the air, shouting.

"It's me!" I yell over the side, waving excitedly at him, but he just scratches his head.

I continue towards the sea for a while before turning to fly over the house for a second time, hoping if I get a little lower, Emrys will know it's me.

I've always known my house is bizarre-looking, but it looks even more peculiar when viewed from above. I know it's a special house, despite all its problems – Pa tells me that often enough – but now something about its appearance sends a shockwave through my body.

The wind drops and I descend to fifty feet or so above the house.

This can't be right.

My overactive imagination must be getting the better

of me again.

Watch your height, Wren.

I tug on one of the cords and coax the Phoenix back up into the air, allowing time for my brain to make sense of what I just saw.

This explains everything.

I need to get home.

I need to get home now. Any thought of escape will have to wait for another day.

I tear back towards the strait and towards the middle of the water where it will be at its deepest, my mind whizzing. Did I really just see what I thought I did? It's too ridiculous. Too unbelievable. I force myself to concentrate. I have to land this thing or I'll find myself in the churchyard with Ma.

I prepare to land, knowing only that I have to keep the Phoenix level and avoid catching the wings in the water. I pull on the cord that controls my height, and begin my descent, but realise with alarm that I'm drifting to the left. I hit a little air pocket and drop about twenty feet.

Dark clouds roll in towards me. The Phoenix rattles and I drop again. I glance at the network of control cords and am horrified to see that one of them is fraying near where it feeds through its pulley. I carefully pull on the threadbare cord to lower myself in a controlled way towards the water.

It snaps in my hand.

The severed cord thrashes about like a serpent.

The Phoenix pitches forward.

I hit the sea.

My face smashes against the front of my coracle. I open my mouth to scream but am swallowed up by the sea and rapidly sucked beneath its surface in a twisting, tumbling tangle of coracle, timber, silk and feathers. The sound of rushing water becomes more muffled as I float gently down towards the seabed.

I open my eyes.

The water around me is turning red.

I'm bleeding!

Swim, Wren!

Every part of me pulsates with pain. I tear my glasses from my face, and a fresh cloud of blood surrounds me.

The strange, disconnected voice comes again, reassuring me now. I close my eyes and allow my broken body to sink.

A firm hand grabs me by my arm. I open my eyes and look around blearily. Medwyn must have come to rescue me. But there's no one here. My eyes close again, and I'm lured by the strange echoing sound of deep water to fall back to sleep.

I feel myself being dragged upwards, up and up towards a bright light above. Soon I burst through the surface of the water, and an invisible hand holds my head up. I'm gasping for air, choking out sea water. I look around through unfocused eyes.

I'm all alone in the middle of the strait. There's no hand holding my chin or gripping my arm, yet it throbs as if strong fingers have only recently been clutching it.

The sea is choppy now and waves begin to smack against my cheeks. Dark, heavy clouds gather above, ready to empty their contents on to the water. And me.

Nothing makes any sense. I must have hit my head harder than I thought when I crashed. *Think!* I blink hard, forcing my eyes to focus. My upturned coracle is close by, bobbing up and down on the surface of the water. I begin a slow swim towards it, fighting against the sea as it tries to draw me back into its depths, Aunty Efa's heavy leather coat weighing me down, but I daren't wriggle out of it and discard it; it's one of her favourites. I keep swimming in this strange dream-like state, but somehow manage to reach the coracle and, with every ounce of strength left in my body, haul myself up and drape myself over it. Only when I'm out of the water do

I realise how cold it is. And how cold I am.

I curl up in a ball, close my eyes and allow the world to become dark.

Chapter Nineteen

I don't know how long I've been asleep, but I wake with a jolt to the sudden feeling that my head is about to explode. I cover my eyes with my hands to try to block out the light that's clawing its way in through my eyelids. I don't feel cold any more. In fact, I'm so hot, I'm drenched in sweat.

A hand touches my arm. "Are you awake, Wren?"

I peer at the voice through my fingers.

Aunty Efa?

I must be home. But how did I get here?

I try to speak, but my voice comes out more like a dry croak.

"It's all right," she says. "No, no, don't make a fuss. Be a big girl now."

She's too late, and as tears roll down my cheeks, the skin around my eyes seems to burst into flames.

She touches my face with a small handkerchief. "There, there, dear," she says, dabbing a little too harshly at my cheek. "You've taken quite a battering. Dr Williams has been over. He's done the best he can. In fact, he says you should be as good as new in no time. Just a few battle scars, but that's to be expected."

Battle scars?

"What?" I whisper.

"From your glasses. They caused a few little cuts here and there, but nothing that won't fade with time."

Aunty Efa is coming more into focus. The smell of her steam makes me feel sick.

"And you took quite a blow to your head, judging by the egg you have up there!"

I gasp as a memory of what happened floods my mind. The flight. It worked! I flew! But then the crash. The icy water that pulled me down to its depths. The

160

upturned hull of the coracle. The intense cold.

"Does Pa know?" I whisper, my head thudding with each word. He was right, after all. I was a fool to think I could fly. Everything he said about me was right.

"Yes, he does."

"And is he furious?" My whole plan, if you could call it a plan, had been to escape from Pa, and now I've made things a hundred times worse. How will I ever get away from him now? How will I stop him locking me up?

"Well, yes, he is actually, and you've done an excellent job of proving him right. But he's even more furious with that stupid boy."

"Medwyn is not stupid," I growl. "I asked him to help me."

"That is irrelevant. He should have known better. He's been round a few times, asking after you, and your father's sent him off with a flea in his ear. As if he thinks he'll get any thanks for pulling you out of the water."

"Medwyn saved me?"

"If you can call it that, and only because he didn't want to end up in Beaumaris Gaol facing manslaughter charges!"

"So he saved my life?"

"Well, that would be an exaggeration. He rowed a boat out to you and dragged you and your mangled flying machine back to the shore. And then brought you back here."

"So he saved me," I whisper.

She sniffs. "And I won't say anything about the coat."

"Sorry about that."

"And the dresses."

"Oh, so you noticed," I say. "But you have so many, Aunty Efa. I didn't think you'd miss one or two."

"Of course I noticed. Do you think I'm a complete fool? I didn't say anything because I didn't want to make things worse between you and your pa."

"Thank you," I whisper. I try to smile at her, but that only makes my face hurt, so I take her hand and squeeze it instead.

Medwyn rescued me and brought me home, knowing what a reception he'd get from my family. I pull my eiderdown over my head but that only makes my face hurt, so I throw it back off again.

"I just wanted to fly away," I wail. "Far away from Pa and the Aireys. I didn't want to cause all this trouble."

"Oh, dear God, so that's the reason for all this. I told him his plan for you and that blasted institution was the most ridiculous idea."

She starts the business of readying her wheelchair to leave the room, creating a cloud of steam that consumes us both. She spins round and heads towards the door, clearly having decided our conversation is over.

"And is the Phoenix ruined?" I whisper, wanting to ask a hundred more questions but not wishing to hear her answers.

"I believe so," she says, reaching forward to pull my bedroom door open.

"Oh," I say. At least it wasn't left in the water, to be washed out to sea and never seen again. She chugs out of the room and trundles noisily down the corridor towards the lift.

I lie in bed listening to the sounds of my house, its strange rhythmic beat and odd vibrations. Light streams through my curtains and I realise I've no idea what time of day it is.

As the hours pass, the details of what happened flood back to me, including what I saw when I flew over my house. And what I saw when I was down in the cellar – the thing that was being prodded by Pa and his razor-sharp tools. I lie still, my mind whirring. I know I didn't imagine either of those things. I think too about what Medwyn does in our house. How he keeps our furnace going. The time has come to talk to him, and perhaps even Emrys too.

I spend a week in bed with Aunty Efa and Pa watching me like a pair of hawks, ready to pounce should I try to creep out of the house. Pa hasn't shipped me off to the institution yet, despite his earlier threats. Lying in bed with nothing to do has given me plenty of time to think about what I did. Pa was right all along. I am a fool. I never think things through and have always had stupid ideas way above my station. Who did I think I was to believe I could fly? I'm just a girl. I'm just Wren. Nothing more.

I don't blame Pa for wanting to lock me up.

Every night I'm plagued by memories of what happened, of the stomach-lurching feeling of falling from the sky and the impact of hitting the water. Why didn't I learn from what happened to Ma? What was I thinking? And now I'm so worried about what's going on with my house, but I'm too battered and bruised to do anything about it.

Aunty Efa surreptitiously removed the mirror from my room that first day, but as soon as I'm able I creep down the corridor and look at myself in Pa's wardrobe mirror. I don't think about what I look like most days; I'm just a bit small and scruffy, with a determined chin. But I'm not prepared for the shock of seeing the damage I've done to my face. Everything's so swollen it's difficult to see exactly what's going on, but it's immediately obvious that my "protective glasses" have inflicted the most damage, with each of the bottle bottoms having left jagged cuts below and above each eye. My eyelids are so swollen you can barely see my eyes. My cheeks, normally ruddy from all the time I spend on the water, are now a dozen shades of red, yellow, orange and purple, with another giant bruise running from my forehead all the way down to my collarbone. A protruding lump above my right eye gives the impression I'm growing a small horn.

I slink back to my room, trying not to cry.

Aunty Efa promises me the swelling and bruising will go down eventually. She called in Mrs Jenkins from the chemist in Beaumaris to apply balms to accelerate the healing process but warned some of my scars might remain for life. Mrs Jenkins seems to be enjoying the daily application of oil of earthworm, foul-smelling vinegary poultices and, the worst of them all, a horse-dung tonic. My inner fire extinguished, I just lie back and let her slather her horrible balms all over my face. After one of these sessions, a memory returns to me. The memory of a smell in the ice house. The smell reminds me of whatever it was Emrys had in his little bowl, but the thought flits out of my mind as sleep overcomes me.

Aunty Efa mentioned, in one of her nicer moments, that scars are the evidence of an interesting life. Ma had plenty of them, and I think she was pretty proud of them; she said they were the marks of a life lived to the full.

With all the bustling, balms and warm compresses, I haven't had a chance to send a message to Medwyn. I can't imagine how he must be feeling. I want to thank him for saving me, to tell him it wasn't his fault.

My opportunity to slip out of the house arrives sooner than expected. Pa mentioned he has a meeting in Bangor this morning, and that Aunty Efa would be in charge of keeping an eye on me, but I haven't seen her all day. She's been so mysterious recently I can't help wondering what she's up to.

I'm in the justice room enduring a lesson with Tudur and Mr Thomas. It seems even facial injuries and concussion are not enough to get me out writing an essay on Chaucer. I'd rather we were doing something like engineering, learning about the giant machines in the factories of Liverpool, or even mathematics. Tudur has finally got bored of teasing me about my face and is busy trying to show off to Mr Thomas with an essay he's written. We're still not allowed into Pa's study, and he still won't tell us why.

I stare out of the window, hypnotised by the sight of the sea, feeling its call. No one will tell me where my coracle is, or even whether it's repairable.

I spot Aunty Efa out on the lawn, deep in conversation with Emrys, which is strange as she never really talks to him. It's a bright day and the sea is as still as sheet glass. It would be the perfect day for being out on the water – just scudding about, or perhaps even riding the Swellies if I was feeling brave enough. My heart soars at the thought of it. I wonder if Medwyn still has my coracle. Perhaps it isn't too damaged. It might still be seaworthy.

Aunty Efa has finished her conversation with Emrys, chugs round to the back of the house and disappears from sight.

Our lesson ends and Mr Thomas shoves his papers into his satchel and bolts from the room. I lean back and stare at the ceiling, wondering whether today might be the day I get to escape.

"I'm going outside," I say to Tudur.

"No, you're not!" he says. "You're not allowed outside!"

He opens his mouth to call Pa's name.

"There's no point," I hiss. "He's in Bangor. He won't hear you from there."

"Well, I'll tell him when he gets back."

I decide to take a different tack. "I'm just going to see Emrys," I lie. "See what he wants for dinner."

"Well, I'll be watching you," he says. "Through this window. Don't think I won't be."

"Why do you even care what I do?"

"Because I think you should have got into a lot more trouble after what you did. They only didn't shout at you more because they thought you'd killed yourself. If it was up to me, you'd have had a good hiding."

"You ridiculous little boy," I say, standing over his desk, glaring at him, overwhelmed by an urge to kick the pale, skinny shins sticking out from his shorts.

Tudur's shins are saved by a sudden movement of the house. The room quivers and the ornaments tremble like chattering teeth.

"Is it another earthquake?" Tudur whispers, looking about, gripping his desk. I can see he's scared, even though he's trying to hide it.

"I think it's to do with the foundations," I say, trying to sound like *I* know what I'm talking about. "Because the house has been built on soft ground. Or something like that." I realise this might be my perfect excuse to get out of here. "I'll see if Emrys saw anything. As Pa and Aunty Efa aren't around, I'm in charge." And without giving Tudur a chance to reply, I race from the room, down the corridor, into the hallway and out through the front door.

I find Emrys sitting on the ground outside the ice house with his legs crossed. He appears to be in a deep trance.

"Emrys," I say, running up to him, gently nudging one of his bony feet with my boot. "Did you just see something strange?"

He doesn't seem to hear me.

"Emrys?" I say, more urgently this time.

He raises a finger to his lips as if to shush me. "Quiet, child," he says, "for I am listening to the world."

"And when you were listening, did you hear what just happened?" I probably shouldn't be standing over him like this, with my hands on my hips, tapping an impatient foot on the ground.

He shakes his head slowly from one side to the other as he waves me away with a small hand gesture.

I look about. There's no one around. I can't even see any boats or sign of life on the water, so I take my chance and head off towards Medwyn's house.

Chapter Twenty

I find Medwyn in his front garden, rinsing out a worm pail. When he sees me, his eyes widen.

"Oh, Wren!" he says, clapping a hand to his mouth.

"It's not that bad!" My bruised cheeks burn under his scrutiny.

"This is because of the glasses I made for you," he says quietly, placing the pail on the ground.

"Well, it's actually because I decided to try to build a

flying machine," I reply. "And then one of the control cords snapped and it fell out of the sky, and if you hadn't made those glasses, I might have got a fly in my eye, and who knows what would have happened then. I might have had to have an entire eyeball removed, which would have been far worse."

Medwyn smiles. "I've tried to come and see you."

"I know, I'm sorry. They've practically imprisoned me in my own house," I say, trying not to cry. "But I don't blame them this time. What was I thinking, Medwyn, doing something so stupid? And why did I drag *you* into it? And is Aunty Dilys furious about you borrowing her cart?"

"Oh, don't worry about me, or Aunty Dilys. She doesn't let things like that bother her."

"We should all be like Aunty Dilys," I say, forcing a smile. "And thank you for saving my life – you know, for pulling me out of the water and everything." It sounds so dramatic when I say it like that. "I'm sure Pa and Aunty Efa are grateful, even if they haven't said it yet."

"I couldn't exactly have left my best friend to drown!"

My heart soars at his words and I can't help grinning at him, despite it making my cheeks throb. "But still, thank you," I say, wishing I had better words in my head to say how I feel. Looking at him now, I suspect he knows what I mean. I peer past him, into his front garden, wondering if he still has the remains of the Phoenix hidden away somewhere. "Was it ruined?" I ask. "When you dragged it out?"

"Not totally. It came apart when you hit the water, but all the parts were intact. Everything was just a bit battered and soggy." He smiles at me. "Like its pilot!"

"And my coracle?" I say, peering behind him towards the lean-to at the side of the house. I can't see much in there, apart from an upturned dingy and a stack of logs.

"It wasn't as bad as you'd expect, considering how hard you hit the water."

"And is it here? I heard you dragged it back in."

"Um, no, not exactly."

"But where is it then?"

"I'm not entirely sure. Someone took it away."

My heart sinks. "Pa?"

"No, someone else. Someone I didn't recognise. They wouldn't take no for an answer. They said it was on behalf of your Aunty Efa."

I bite my lip crossly. What was Aunty Efa doing taking the remains of the Phoenix away? It isn't hers to take!

Medwyn shuffles from one foot to the other, his hands deep in his pockets. "I shouldn't ask you this with everything going on, but did you see anything strange while you were up there?" He says it casually, in an offhand sort of way, but he doesn't take his eyes off me.

"I saw a lot when I was up there," I say, still unsure how much to tell him. I haven't talked to anyone about any of it yet. No one's asked me what it was like to fly. How it felt to soar in the sky like a bird, or when I reached a pocket of air and then dropped with my heart in my mouth until I found the next corridor of air to lift me up again. What it felt like when I hit the water.

I've wanted to tell them all that I understand now why Ma wanted to do it. Why she took such a risk.

But I know I'll never do it again.

The thought fills me with terror.

"So what was it you saw then, apart from the sky and the birds, and then the seabed?"

"I did see something a little strange," I whisper. "But you know what my imagination's like."

"You shouldn't listen to your pa," Medwyn says, frowning. "Maybe there are some things he doesn't want you to see."

I know now he's right. It's just if you're told something often enough, you begin to believe it.

"And?"

"There was something," I say. "You know everything that's going on with the house: the cracks, the movement, the strange noises. But this was something a bit different."

"Did what you saw help to explain what's going on?"

"Oh, I don't know," I say. "It's so ridiculous I can't even put it into words. Our house does look a bit unusual from the front and the back, and from the side. But from above…"

I suddenly realise that Medwyn knows far more than he's been letting on.

"You know, don't you?" I say, trying to contain the little ball of anger that's just ignited inside me. "Why didn't you tell me, Medwyn? Why did you have to let me find out like that?"

"I'm sorry! I just didn't know how or when to tell you. And to start with I thought you were in on it. You are one of *them*, after all."

He sees the look on my face. "But I know you're not like your pa. We were just doing what we had to do to keep it safe."

"We?" I say crossly.

He doesn't reply.

"Do you mean Emrys? Does he know about all this too?"

"Yes, he does."

I nod. "Of course he does. And if there's a problem with the house that Pa hasn't been dealing with properly,

then I'm going to have to instead. I must go and see it,"
I say.

Medwyn nods. "He's there now. He's been tending to
it. To its wounds, you see."

"The wounds Pa's been inflicting?" I whisper.

"Yes, those." Medwyn's lips are tight.

"But what was he doing? I saw him pull something off
it, some sort of dusty metal."

"Well, that's the problem, see. It isn't just some dusty
old metal. It's gold. Welsh gold. The best in the world."

I gasp. This explains everything. We're sitting on a
gold mine. Of course Pa was never going to do the right
thing.

As we walk back quickly along the edge of the water
towards my house, I remember the book Aunty Efa
wanted me to pass to her in the justice room, and how
it had fallen open on the story of Lludd and Llefelys. I
now wonder if *she* also knows more than she's letting on,
that she hasn't closed her eyes and ears to Pa's actions,
after all.

Chapter Twenty-One

At the ice house we head straight for the giant, empty bowl that once held the household's ice. Emrys's small pile of possessions is as it was last time, his blankets folded neatly and his slippers placed to the side of his makeshift bed. It's as warm in here as it was before.

The sconce on the wall is lit, suggesting Emrys was only recently here. The small door I'd seen him emerging through last time is ajar. "So this is the other way in," I say.

Medwyn nods. "The answer to everything lies down here." He glances back towards the ladder, as if checking no one has followed us. "It's dark down here, so stay close."

He ducks as he passes through the doorway and I follow him into a low, narrow tunnel. It's even warmer down here than in the ice house. We follow it for some time until we reach a fork, then take an even narrower tunnel that leads to another wooden door.

Medwyn steps to one side and I pull the door open and walk into a dimly lit cave, the same place I'd followed Pa and the Aireys into. It takes a while for my eyes to adjust to the gloom. It's dark in here except for a diffuse red glow coming from the centre of the space. The stuffy air resonates with the steady boom of a heartbeat.

"Would you like to meet her properly?" Medwyn says.

He holds out a hand. I don't take it but follow him instead towards the scaffold.

"Is it what I think it is?" I whisper.

"*She* is," he says.

When I was up in the Phoenix I'd realised that our house was no ordinary house. In that brief moment, from that elevated position, I'd seen that my home was the shape of a beast. Every sensible cell in my brain told me I was being ridiculous, that I was "imagining things" like Pa says, that the excitement of flying must have affected my ability to think straight. But there is no denying that I am now looking up at the low-slung, gently heaving belly of a creature so vast it defies belief. And in a far corner of the cave rests a giant, scaled leg ending in an enormous clawed foot. It has been shackled. The heaving belly has an eight-foot patch of pink, raw-looking skin that is entirely devoid of scales.

"How could he?" I say.

"Is this what you thought you saw, from above?"

"Yes. I always knew our house was a strange shape," I say, "but I didn't expect it to have a forked tail. Or a ridge of sharp spines running along its roof." I squint at the creature. "She's alive?"

"Only just."

"So this beast is below and above my house?"

"This beast *is* your house," Medwyn replies simply.

My heart misses a beat. I reach up and touch the underside of the belly, as I would to reassure an injured animal. The heavy boom-boom of the creature's heart seems to settle, just a little.

"I think she likes you," Medwyn says.

I run my fingers along her warm skin, feeling my touch calming her.

"And she is a dragon."

I say the words to myself as if they're just simple words. As if I don't appreciate their power.

"Yes, she's a dragon," Medwyn says. "And she's trapped. And your pa's doing everything to keep it that way."

For a moment I wonder if this is all a part of my concussion, that I'm having some sort of hallucination. That I'm actually in bed and Aunty Efa is by my side, sponging my forehead. But this is real. I'm surrounded by smoke and heat and the acrid smell that creeps into our rooms through our fireplaces. And I have the thick, spongy skin of this poor creature, this dragon, under my fingertips.

"So we need to release her," I say, "before she dies."

"Well, it isn't quite that simple," Medwyn replies, "because, you see, the dragon and your house have become one. To separate one from the other will destroy either the dragon, or your house."

"Well, we'll have to destroy my house then!" I cry.

What was Pa thinking? Our house clearly doesn't belong to us, and he thought he could somehow make it so by singing stupid songs about some long-dead ancestor and obsessing about my chin. A sudden thought hits me. This must be why he wanted to send me away to the Aireys' institution. He knows what I'm like. He knew I'd want to help her if I found out about her. It was nothing to do with me going out in my coracle. It was all just an excuse.

My eyes fill with tears. Tears for this poor creature – this poor, desperate, beautiful beast that is trapped within my house. And for me too, and for my poor, stupid Pa. "However did this happen?" I wail.

"Oh, my dear Wren of the house, it is a long and complicated story."

I spin round and find Emrys standing behind us, smiling at me in the way he does, leaning on his long stick.

"And you knew about this too?" I say, even though I know the answer.

"My child, I have known about this situation for many years."

"And how long has she been here?" I whisper.

"I would like to share a story with you," Emrys says. "It is a story as old as Wales, told by the ancients, but only ever sung to those with the ears to hear. Let us sit, for this story cannot be told in haste."

And so, as instructed, I perch on a small rock close to the belly of the dragon that lies beneath my house and listen as Emrys begins his tale.

Chapter Twenty-Two

The Story of the Egg

"Many hundreds of years ago," Emrys begins, "there lived a Welsh chieftain named Gruffudd ap Bleddyn ap Llewelyn. He ruled this land in the time of the English king, Edward I."

"I know him," I say. "This is the ancestor Pa always goes on about!"

Emrys nods. "Unfortunately for the Welsh, King Edward had set himself the task of conquering Wales, forcing its people to submit to English rule. Gruffudd ap Bleddyn ap Llewelyn was a loyal supporter of the Prince of Gwynedd, and, as was his duty, he mustered a small army to help defend our land from the invading English."

"I remember Pa talking about this too," I say, wishing I'd listened to his lectures now, about how Gruffudd ap Bleddyn ap Llewelyn and his men had fought the English with such courage.

"But your ancestor had other problems that were occupying his attention."

"Pa says there was a battle, I think, and that he was victorious," I say, not feeling entirely sure of my facts.

"Well, it's possible there was a battle, but I'm not aware of that," Emrys says. "You see, he was distracted from the business of war by a strange discovery. He and his men had concealed themselves in a cave deep beneath the Crib Goch ridge, where they could light their fires and rest before they faced the English in battle. And that is when they made their discovery. It was an egg, see. A boy soldier was the first to lay eyes on it, and everyone was quite perplexed by the sight because no one had seen anything quite like it before."

"And this is connected with what's happening here now?" I say.

"It is indeed," Emrys replies. "The events that happened in that cave so long ago explain everything that's happening now. It is said the young boy approached the egg with some caution. And who can blame him, considering its size!"

"How big was it?" I whisper.

"From all accounts it was the size of a young child." Emrys glances about as if the walls around us might have ears. "But there was something even stranger about it." He lowers his voice, and I lean in to hear him. "You see, the boy made the mistake of touching the egg with the tips of his fingers, and the heat of the egg made him leap back in horror." He looks at me through bright eyes. "Its heat melted the skin on the boy's fingertips. It's said he made a terrible fuss. And then the young, and, let it be said, rather foolish, Gruffudd ap Bleddyn ap Llewelyn was summoned." He stops. "Do you mind if we call him 'Gruff' for short? His name is such a terrible mouthful."

I shake my head.

"So your ancestor, whom we are now calling 'Gruff', came to investigate. *What monstrosity is contained within this shell?* he shouted. *It is an abomination!* And with that he wrapped the egg in a sheepskin, so as to protect *his* fingers from its heat, and lifted it above his head and swung the hot package towards a nearby stalagmite. But there was a young man in their midst who didn't like Gruff's plan to destroy the egg, and he leaped between Gruff and the stalagmite, allowing his body to prevent the egg from shattering into a thousand pieces."

"And it survived?" I whisper.

"It did indeed, and after his rage subsided Gruff was persuaded by the young man that the egg might one day be a valuable commodity. Now, your great-great-great, however many times, grandfather was not known for being the wisest of men, but that day he chose to listen to someone wiser than him. That man was Owain. The many-greats grandfather of Medwyn."

I glance over at Medwyn, who is whispering words of comfort to the dragon's belly but clearly listening to us.

"On the advice of Owain, Gruff saw to it that the egg was wrapped in skins and carried with care to the surface. He was quite distracted, you see, by the thought of the great wealth this egg might one day bring him, and he buried the egg on a parcel of land on Anglesey that overlooked the Menai Strait and the mountains beyond, and covered it over with straw. Soon after, he built a small timber structure above it to protect it."

"And it was still alive?" I say, horrified at the idea of

an egg being taken from its rightful place. "But might its parent have come back for it?"

"Who knows?" Emrys says. "Perhaps after laying the egg, their work was done. And the problem for Gruff, which he was not aware of at the time, was that an egg such as that takes many lifetimes to hatch. Far longer than the lifetime of a chieftain, even if he had lived to a ripe old age. But young Gruff got himself killed soon afterwards, not long after he'd laid the foundation stones for your house."

"In a battle with the English?"

Emrys shakes his head. "I believe it was in a brawl over a horse."

"How do you know all this? You're talking about it as if you were there!"

Emrys blushes slightly.

I squint in the half-light at his paper-thin skin and deep lines around his eyes. People often refer to him as Emrys the Ancient. I wonder exactly how ancient he is.

"So what happened after Gruff died?" I say, shaking the notion out of my head.

"Well, Gruff's son, Dewi, inherited the piece of land containing the egg, and he too decided the egg was worth protecting. It was still hot, you see. And so Dewi, son of Gruff, continued his father's work and built a heavily fortified house over the egg, with walls that were eight feet thick."

"My house," I say. "Is that what he built?"

"You have a quick mind, young Wren. Yes, your many-greats grandfather, Dewi ap Gruffudd ap Bleddyn, built your house over the egg. It was to conceal it, see, and to protect it too, as rumours of its value, should it hatch, persisted. Of course, not one person imagined for a moment what beast might be growing within it."

"But doesn't an egg need a parent to sit on it, to keep it warm until it hatches?"

"But what if the land becomes the parent? Perhaps the egg has all it needs by being buried deep within the rich Welsh soil."

"And so it lay beneath the ground, taking everything it needed from the soil, like a tulip bulb?" I ask.

Emrys nods. "And it lay there for so long that everyone eventually forgot it had ever been there. A long-lost secret lying silently beneath your house, waiting for its time. An egg such as that takes hundreds of years to hatch, and then, when it finally did, it *still* wasn't ready to join the world. You see, a young dragon will remain in a state of deep slumber as it continues to grow. And they grow so slowly, Wren, for it takes time for each detail to become just perfect. Each scale is like a piece of fine jewellery, each muscle the branch of an ancient oak, each claw a great stalactite. And so this beautiful beast grew in its soporific state, but, like a young plant left in its pot too long, it became entangled within that which protected it – your house, with its tall tower and eight-foot-thick walls. And as it grew, every part of it, above what you see here, grew into and around the stonework of your house, until the two became one."

I shiver as I absorb the enormity of what Emrys has just told me. I turn back, wide-eyed, to Medwyn. He's still with the dragon but is watching me carefully.

"And with time, parts of that sleeping giant became stone, so confused was this jumble of body, scale and stone."

"My house is a dragon," I say, quietly allowing it to sink in properly.

"Well, not exactly. Your house is a dragon that has inadvertently become petrified, in parts."

"A dragon turned to stone," I say, "in parts," as if explaining it to myself.

"And the problem we have now," Emrys says, "is that she is ready to fly, and your father and the Aireys are doing everything to stop that happening. You see, they're quite pleased to be sitting on a gold mine."

I realise I've never heard him say quite so many words

in one go.

"Well, we just have to work out how to help her escape, even if it means destroying the house," I say.

Emrys nods and we sit in silence for a while. My house is a dragon that has been asleep for hundreds of years, and that is readying itself to fly.

"This explains everything," I say. "The way the house moves and settles and sometimes seems to sigh. The strange twisting corridors and undulating floors. The unexplained hot spots. The smoke!"

Emrys nods.

"But if we could just do something to keep the Aireys away," I say, my mind racing, "then the dragon would be safe?"

"But look at her, Wren," Medwyn says. "Can she stay like this forever? Trapped? Risking being picked at by whoever hears about her?"

"But to release her will destroy the house," I say, worrying to what extent Pa will go to avoid seeing his precious home in ruins.

"The alternative is for the dragon to perish," he says.

"And, you see, it has begun to call," Emrys adds.

"To call?" I look at them, my eyes wide. "I've heard it! I've heard it over and over again, but I didn't know what it was, and Pa kept telling me it was all a figment of my imagination!"

"It's more of a song really," Emrys says. "And of course you wouldn't know what it was. She's calling to the mountains, see."

"But unfortunately they're not answering," Medwyn adds. "And as she began her life in the belly of the mountains, she is the child of the mountains. She cannot fly until they respond. Until they call to her."

"And why are they not responding?" I say, wondering how a mountain can possibly reply to a song, but deciding to go along with what they're saying.

"Because they can't hear her," Medwyn says. "She's weak and her song simply isn't loud enough."

I think through everything they've just told me. "So we have a dragon trapped underneath my house. Her strength is being depleted by what Pa and the Aireys are doing to her. And she needs to be set free, but she's weak from having her scales removed.

"And to be able to escape she needs the mountains to respond to her song, but because she's so weak they can't hear her. And if she stays here, she'll die. But if she escapes, she'll destroy my house." I look from one to the other of them. "Is that everything?"

They nod.

"Oh, it's all so terribly sad, Wren, to hear her cry out

like that," Emrys says.

"And what will happen if the mountains don't respond?"

"Then she will surely die."

"She should be free," I say, "skimming the mountain peaks, soaring above Caernarfon Bay, setting the sky alight at dusk." I think hard. "So if the mountains hear her song, and respond, then there's a chance she might live?"

Medwyn nods.

A hot rage surges through my belly. "And not one person thought to tell me about this! Am I the only one who doesn't know?"

"No," Medwyn says. "I don't think your Aunty Efa knows, or Tudur."

I raise an eyebrow but say nothing about Aunty Efa.

Emrys taps my knee. "And you see, Wren, just as you are descended from Gruff, so Medwyn is descended from Owain, the one who saved the egg. And Medwyn's inheritance is to keep it alive."

"And that's why you were always in my house? Were you feeding it? Was that what it was?"

"Well, sort of," Medwyn says. "I've been keeping her fire alight, until she's strong enough to make her own flames."

Emrys smiles at Medwyn, like a proud father.

"So it was nothing to do with keeping our house warm," I whisper, my cheeks burning.

"You mustn't chastise yourself," Emrys says gently. "Great efforts have been taken to keep this under wraps."

"But why did it have to be kept secret?"

"To protect her, until she's ready to fly," Medwyn says.

"I would have protected her," I say crossly. "And if you don't mind me saying, you haven't exactly done the best job yourselves!"

Medwyn's cheeks now flush. "We had to do what was right for her. You might have sided with your pa. You are one of them, after all."

"Only in name," I hiss. "I'd have worked out a way to stop him if I'd known about it."

"And we worried you had enough going on with your ma," Emrys says kindly.

"You still should have told me," I mutter.

"We know that now," Medwyn says quietly. "I'm sorry."

The boom-boom of the dragon's heart begins to falter.

"Is she all right?" I say, spinning to look her. Her belly is trembling.

"No," Emrys says. "She is most troubled, and if she

doesn't fly soon, then she will perish. It is that simple."

"Does it have to be *her* who sings to the mountains?" I say, a thought stirring in the back of my mind. "Could someone else sing on her behalf?"

Emrys looks at me and shakes his head. "But that would take some projection. I don't know anyone who could carry their voice all the way to the mountains, however good a singer they might be."

"Well, maybe *one* person couldn't do it," I say. "But what about a whole choir? Or even several choirs? How many are there on Anglesey? There must be dozens! Their combined singing might just be enough for the mountains to hear."

"It might work," Medwyn says, glancing at Emrys.

"And Pa will help," I say. "That's the least he can do to put things right. He could gather his singing group together, and all the others in the area. His voice alone is pretty powerful."

"But will he help?" Medwyn says. "He's been doing everything in his power to keep the dragon imprisoned and his gold mine undisturbed. And he'll be left without his precious house to live in!"

"But it isn't his house, is it?" I say. "It's a dragon. And a dragon belongs to no one but itself!"

Chapter Twenty-Three

I look everywhere for Pa. The study is locked and there's no reply when I bang on the door. I try the justice room, but only find Tudur in there sitting alone at Ma's desk doing some schoolwork. I look everywhere else, but the house seems deserted. I return to the study and hammer on the door. Pa must be hiding in there.

I push my ear to the door and hear an anguished sob. I kick the door as hard as I can, my heart thundering.

"Pa!" I call. "It's Wren."

A shuffling sound comes from inside the room and I hear the click of someone turning a key in the lock. I push the door open in time to see Pa shuffling back across the room, all thin and bent like one of the Aireys. He slumps into his old leather armchair, picks up his glass of wine and tips what's left of it into his mouth. An empty bottle lies on the floor at his feet. His eyes are bloodshot and his hair is wild. With an unsteady hand, he places the glass on the arm of his chair and raises his eyes to look up at me.

My rage is briefly diminished when I notice a long, gaping crack in the far wall of the study. It's so wide a person could squeeze through it. Pa's made a desperate attempt to block it up with a chair piled high with books, but the wound stretches up far higher than he was able to reach, leaving an open crevice at the top.

I glance at it nervously. "Pa, we have to talk."

He hurls his wine glass at the opposite wall and it shatters into thousands of tiny fragments. "This is it," he says, tears rolling down his cheeks. "This is the end, Wren."

"It depends on how you look at it," I hiss.

"We appear to have a problem with the house," he slurs, "in case you haven't noticed."

195

"I can hardly fail to have noticed," I snap. "And I think it may be more of a problem with what lies beneath it."

"Ah, so you know then," he says. "My clever daughter has worked out what our little problem is."

"Two things," I say, my hands on my hips. "Firstly, this is not a *little* problem, and, secondly, how long did you think you could hide the fact that we have a dragon trapped under our house, Pa? The dragon *is* our house! We are living in a dragon! How could you think that would ever go away?" I'm shouting now, my hands shaking. "How could you have ignored this? Or, even worse, tried to make money out of it? And all the while thinking the whole thing would be cured by going on and on about how important our ancestors were, when they were nothing more than egg thieves!" I shout the last bit at him.

He pulls a handkerchief from his pocket and wipes his nose. "I'm sorry," he weeps. "Your ma would have known what to do if she'd still been here. She'd have sorted everything out."

"But she isn't here, is she? And what have you done to sort things out? Steal the dragon's scales! How could you, Pa?"

He hangs his head. "But it's just an animal. It wouldn't have felt anything."

196

"She's a living dragon!" I shout. "Of course she'd have felt it!"

"Oh, now you're being ridiculous!" He refuses to meet my eyes.

"How would you feel if someone pulled out your fingernails?" I hiss.

"I didn't think about it like that," he says sulkily.

"Well, you should have."

"But I did it for us, Wren. If it escapes, we're ruined! We'll have nothing left!"

"The house will be ruined, but *we* won't be."

"But it's our inheritance! Our responsibility. Its foundations were laid by Gruffudd ap Bleddyn ap Llewelyn, with the certainty that future generations would live here forever."

"You clearly know nothing about him," I say.

He looks at me blearily.

"And is that why you wanted to send me away? So I wouldn't get involved?" I shout. "Is that what this was all about?"

Pa sobs. "Well, it was partly that, yes, but…" He stops to blow his nose. "I didn't want you to die, Wren! You're always doing such stupid, dangerous things." He begins to sob uncontrollably. "I couldn't lose you as well!"

"But I was never going to die, Pa! I'm careful and I

work things out. I listen to other people and take advice. I'm not reckless!" Part of me wants to hug him, but I'm still furious with him. "But you have a chance to make things right," I say quietly, crouching down in front of him.

"It's too late," he says, weeping. "Too late for everything."

"No, it's not. Listen to me. I'm assuming you've heard the dragon singing. That noise you always said was a *figment of my imagination*?"

Pa nods and stifles a sob.

"And do you know why she was singing?"

Pa shakes his head.

"You see, Pa, she wasn't singing. She was calling for help. Calling to the mountains. She's their child and she can't fly until they respond. And because she's trapped within these walls, they can't hear her!"

Pa raises his head and looks up at me through swollen eyes. "I didn't know that's what it was doing."

"But you chose not to find out," I hiss. "You could have asked Emrys. Or Medwyn."

"Meddlesome pair," Pa mutters.

"They were protecting the dragon," I shout. "As you should have been!"

"Well, it's all too late now. Everything is lost. The

house. Us. The dragon."

"But that's the thing," I say in more of a conciliatory tone. "It isn't too late. And I'm going to give you the chance to put things right."

"By putting things right, you mean destroying our house?"

"Our house is destroyed already," I say. "But we have to set the dragon free, Pa. We let her die or we set her free. Either way our house is ruined."

"But we could keep repairing the cracks," Pa says. "If she doesn't get any bigger."

"You mean if you allow her to die," I hiss.

Pa stares at his feet, and I stand over him, looking down on him.

"You can help her," I say quietly.

"And how do you propose I do that?"

"We need to help the mountains hear her, Pa! But I can't do this without you. You are the best singer I know. And your choir can make quite a racket. We need to gather *all* the singers on the island. Can you do that? Can you get them to meet here tomorrow morning? Could you all sing together instead of in competition?"

Pa shakes his head. "It doesn't work like that, Wren."

"Well, tomorrow you are going to sing together," I say firmly. "You are going to go out and ask every singer you know on Anglesey, and further afield if possible, to meet in the front garden tomorrow at midday." I say it slowly and clearly as if I'm talking to a small child. "Tell each of them to spread the word, to ask everyone they know. We need to create a resounding song, a song that the mountains cannot fail to hear. It's the dragon's only chance."

Chapter Twenty-Four

I lie awake all night, my mind alive with a thousand thoughts. I told Aunty Efa everything when she returned home last night. She said she'd worked most of it out already, or at least had an inkling of what was going on after re-reading "Lludd and Llefelys" from the *Mabinogion*, the story of two dragons, one red and one white, trapped beneath a hillock near Beddgelert. Despite promising to keep her nose out of Pa's activities in return for money, she'd borrowed his keys and sent Alis down to the cellar to investigate. If she was feeling guilty about her role in keeping the dragon imprisoned, she didn't admit to that. She simply said how much she hated the house and how the memories of Ma were just too much for her to cope with most days. She said she wouldn't miss any of it if my plan works.

She's still being elusive and won't say where she's been to each day. I've asked her to help tomorrow, but she said she's too busy. I shouldn't be surprised really.

Pa has sent messages to every choir and singing group in the area, requesting their presence for an *Impromptu and Extraordinary Spectacle of Song*. I think he's just going along with it to try to make amends. I said we should take our most treasured possessions out of the house in the morning, but he'd laughed in a slightly deranged way. I know he doesn't believe my plan will work; he thinks that the dragon won't be set free and the house won't be destroyed, but that I might forgive him for helping me try.

I worry this won't work, that I've made a terrible mistake, that the dragon will perish whatever we do, or that we'll release her and she'll go on a rampage, killing everyone in sight; she is a wild animal, after all. It hadn't even occurred to me that she might be dangerous.

I whisper to Ma from under my blankets, pleading with her to talk to me, to tell me I'm doing the right thing, but she doesn't seem to be listening.

Soon the pale light of the morning begins to creep into my room. I climb out of bed, my heart heavy, tiptoe across the floor, draw the curtains back and look across the water towards the mountains. It looks like someone has sprinkled icing sugar over their craggy peaks during the night. I sigh. They're just mountains. Great slabs of rock. Nothing more. Of course they won't sing. I mutter under my breath, cursing my stupid imagination all over again.

We eat breakfast in silence, none of us certain what is going to happen today. Pa's eyes are even more swollen than yesterday. Tudur keeps glaring at me, as if everything is my fault, his arm wrapped protectively round his bulging satchel. I smile at him, but he looks away and shakes his head.

I reach over to Pa and touch his hand. He bristles slightly but doesn't pull it away. "It's just a house," I whisper. "We can build another one. One that isn't full of cracks. Or terrible secrets."

"But it's more than that, isn't it?" he says quietly, sounding like a very different pa to just a few days ago.

"It's our memories too. You know. Of your ma."

"But she's with *us*, Pa," I say, pressing a hand to my chest. "In our hearts. I think she'll come with us wherever we go."

Pa nods sullenly. Eventually he takes a deep breath. "I've decided we should take a few things outside," he says, glancing around the dining room, "just in case."

"That's a good idea, Pa," I say.

He stares at the uneaten kipper on his plate, his lips tight. "This feels like the last supper."

"Or the last breakfast," Tudur corrects him.

"And have you been down to visit it this morning?" Pa says, his eyes fixed on his place.

"I'm going down to see *her* after breakfast."

"Can I come?" Tudur says, sniffing.

"Yes, of course, we can go together," I reply.

Tudur knows all about the dragon now, but he doesn't know about Pa stealing her scales; he doesn't need to know about that.

Everything feels different down below the cellar, even to yesterday. It isn't quite as warm and smoky, and the boom of the dragon's heart seems less pronounced, and perhaps a little slower. Medwyn and Emrys are with her, whispering to her, reassuring her. Emrys is applying a smelly balm to her damaged skin. I take Tudur's hand and lead him towards the dragon. His eyes are wide and darting about all over the place.

"How is she?" I whisper.

Medwyn shakes his head. "She's ailing, Wren."

I press a reassuring hand to her belly. "Do you think she can hear us?"

"I think she can. We've been talking to her all night, letting her know we're here. And Emrys has been singing to her. She seems to like that."

"You can touch her," I whisper to Tudur.

He reaches up with a small hand and touches her with just his fingertips, as if worried her skin might be on fire.

"We're going to set you free," I whisper. "Today, before the day is done, you'll be soaring over Yr Wyddfa and all of Snowdonia, skimming the waves of Cardigan Bay, flying like a bird!" I correct myself. "Flying like a dragon!" Something about the way her heartbeat seems to settle suggests she understands me or is comforted by my words.

"Is she dangerous?" Tudur says.

"Oh, you mustn't worry about that," Emrys says. "She may be ferocious-looking but she's the gentlest of beasts."

We remain there for a while, whispering to the dragon,

reassuring her. And for just the briefest moment, as we huddle in the stillness of this warm womb-like space, I feel Ma behind my shoulder. The feeling is so strong I twist round, expecting to find her standing behind me, but of course it's just my silly imagination.

"We'd better go," I say eventually. "We need to help Pa prepare for the *Spectacle of Song*!"

"And we'll stay with her. Until it's time," Medwyn says. "To keep her calm."

"But you must get out before, you know, if it looks like our plan's going to work."

"You mustn't worry one jot about us," Emrys says. "We can look after ourselves."

"But what if the Aireys appear? What if they've heard what's happening? They might even try to hurt you!"

A look passes between them. "If they do, I shall show them the sharp end of my stick," Emrys says brightly with a smile that doesn't quite reach his eyes.

And so I leave them with a heavy heart, part of me praying they'll get out of here on time and the other thinking the whole thing is just too fanciful to ever work, and that she'll just perish where she is, trapped in our house forever.

Chapter Twenty-Five

I find Pa on the driveway at the front of the house, his hair wild, shirt tails hanging over his trousers, fussing about with reams of sheet music. Tudur, his hair now sticking out at all angles, runs to join him and starts handing the music out to the assembling singers.

"This is not going to work, Wren," Pa hisses. "It's too ridiculous."

"Well, do you have a better suggestion?" I say, glaring

at him.

He doesn't answer me as we're interrupted by Aunty Dilys and her cart thundering towards us with two of Pa's singing group clinging to the passenger seats.

"I'll be off for more," she shouts, barely giving her white-knuckled passengers time to leap to safety before flicking her whip and tearing back down the drive. I wonder how much Medwyn has told her, but judging by the look of grim determination on her face, I suspect she knows everything.

I leave Pa with his singers and run up to my room to gather a few things. I don't have much that's really important to me: a threadbare dog Ma gave me for my eighth birthday, my sketchbooks and a small selection of books on birds. I shove them into a pillowcase, sling it over my shoulder and head back outside.

I run down to the beach, not feeling much like making conversation with anyone, and instead watch the gathering crowd from a distance. I scan the house, looking for a sign of movement.

The singers arrange themselves into little groups. Pa positions himself in front of everyone, handing out sheets of music, issuing instructions. People are whispering about him, perhaps unsettled by his dishevelled appearance and downbeat demeanour.

They're a competitive lot, with old grudges and scores to settle, and they'll be pleased to have a chance to get together before the Eisteddfod next summer. Everyone's dressed in their Sunday best, and, looking at them now in all their finery, I suddenly realise I haven't seen Aunty Efa since breakfast. Perhaps I should have brought some of her things outside too, but I wouldn't know where to start, and I certainly wouldn't want to waste time rescuing any of her gruesome hats.

Alis and Mrs Edwards are outside too, ready to join in with the singing.

I decide to quickly run back through the house, to check no one's still inside. I sprint up through the garden, under the weeping willows, past the rhododendrons and in through the open front door.

I run into the dining room first. The side table has been set up ready for dinner and a fire is sizzling in the grate. The candelabras have been freshly polished. I check Pa's study, the justice room and the drawing room. They're all empty, apart from the usual detritus of our lives. The drawing room smells of woodsmoke. I breathe it all in, committing every detail to memory. I sit on the settee for just a moment, remembering how Ma used to read to me here when I was little. I say a quiet goodbye to the room and head into the kitchens. A duck sits in a large roasting tin on the table, ready to be put in the oven.

One of the kitchen cats creeps into the pantry. I scoop it up and carry it, wriggling in my arms, as I check the bedrooms and attic rooms. When I'm certain the house is empty, I bolt the back door and run through the house and out of the front door, closing it behind me. The cat leaps from my arms and disappears into a nearby bush.

I suddenly remember the dogs. They definitely weren't in the house, but I don't have time to look for them now as Pa has begun to address the singers. They often take themselves off on walks; I have to trust they're safe.

Pa's done an impressive job of rounding people up. There must be more than a hundred men, women and children now in front of the house, ready to sing for a cause they know nothing about.

The sensible part of me says this can't possibly work.

All I have is hope.

We are the dragon's only chance.

Pa, in his position of choirmaster of St Tysilio's, begins the proceedings. After a quick pep talk to the choir, he begins to sing. His voice is deep and resonant and carries across the garden. After the first verse, other members of his singing group begin to join him, the tenors at first, then the sopranos, the basses and finally the children, their voices rising and weaving together in harmony. And then Pa invites the other singers to join, one group or choir at a time, their voices swelling like a wave, a crescendo building. The song finishes and everyone falls silent.

Nothing happens. The crowd chatters away, oblivious to the real reason they're here. I worry we should have explained everything to them, but they wouldn't have believed us or else just thought Pa had taken leave of his senses.

Pa claps his hands to get everyone's attention. "And now we shall sing the latest composition by Brinley Richards, 'Let the Hills and Vales Resound'. You should all be familiar with this piece."

Tudur hands round more sheets of music, and soon everyone's ready to sing again.

I'm worried about Medwyn and Emrys. Shouldn't they be out by now?

Pa begins again by singing the first verse, and his voice cuts through the air. One by one, the singing groups join him.

Let the hills and vales resound, every heart with rapture bound.

The song sweeps through the air like a tidal wave, surging towards our house, crashing against its walls,

211

lapping at its windows before retreating out to sea.

Our flag doth fly 'neath freedom's sky.

Wake now our song!

Each verse conjures wave after wave of song that batters the walls of my house until it shivers from the top of the tower all the way down to its subterranean roots.

And then a new voice joins our song.

It's coming from the tower – a long, low, mournful lament that becomes more insistent with each beat. It consumes us all, clutching us with warm fingers, holding us in its grip.

It is the song of the dragon, calling to the mountains, calling to be set free.

My house shudders.

What have I begun?

The singers, seeming to notice the strange addition to their song, look up in confusion but continue to sing.

The house trembles.

The ground shakes.

Pa, his eyes red and wild, carries on singing.

The singers continue too, as if transfixed, repeating the first verse now over and over.

The song from the top of the house comes again. The dragon is now singing with *us*, imitating our tune.

And then a great boom ricochets over our heads from

a distant place. For one terrifying moment I fear there's been an explosion at one of the mines. But it comes again and again.

The boom is coming from the mountains.

The mountains are responding to our song!

The house quivers. Then fragments of mortar burst out from the walls and tumble to the ground.

I look about desperately. Where are Medwyn and Emrys?

The house could fall at any second.

I race towards the ice house, throw open the door and leap down the ladder into the empty bowl. I open the door at the far side and run down the long, dark tunnel that leads to the dragon's prison.

I turn a corner and to my horror am met by a mountain of fallen rock.

The tunnel is blocked.

I call out to Medwyn and Emrys and hear a muffled reply.

The ground shudders beneath my feet. Flurries of dust and stone fragments fall on my head. Blinking, I sweep the debris from my face. I don't have time to get help. Without thinking I tear at the pile of stones with my bare hands, praying the roof doesn't collapse on top of me.

"Medwyn!" I shout.

"Get out of here, Wren!" His voice reaches me through the rockfall.

I stop to catch my breath, to allow my heart to settle. And as I pause to listen, I realise they too are scrabbling at the rockfall from the other side. I take a deep breath and carry on. And after what feels like an eternity, we make a small gap in the stones, large enough for me to see Emrys's dusty face on the other side. We continue to tear away at the fallen rocks until we've created a cavity large enough for them to climb through. Emrys has a gash in his forehead, and blood is trickling down his white gown; he must have been hit by a rock. I pass him a handkerchief, which he presses to the wound to stem the bleeding.

Without saying another word we run back through the tunnel, the ground rocking beneath our feet, larger stones now falling around us. The ice house is still intact when we reach it and we race through it, up the ladder, through the lobby and burst out into the bright afternoon light.

Everyone is still singing.

But hundreds of eyes are focused on the top of the tower.

Chapter Twenty-Six

A great resonant boom hurtles towards us from the mountains. The ground quakes. A raised part of the battlements shakes itself free from its mortar and topples down the side of the house like a fallen tooth. The other battlements follow its lead and tumble to the ground, landing in a succession of hefty thuds. The attic windows pop out one by one, making splintering noises as they hit the ground. The walls of the tower begin to bulge, like puffed-up cheeks. Giant stones, still for hundreds of years, follow the lead of the battlements and leap, almost joyously, from the collapsing building, and form a jagged pile on the ground.

Pa runs to me, his eyes streaming.

Everyone is silent now or whispering to each other.

"What have we done?" he wails. "What have *you* done, Wren?"

I swallow hard. "*We've* done the right thing," I hiss, but my voice is lost in the racket of falling masonry.

And so our house disintegrates in a great thundering mess of crashing stone and tearing metal, spewing out the contents of my life on to the lawn. Pa's dragon painting bursts through what was once a window, rises into the air and lands with a crunch on the gravel drive. Next comes a box of Aunty Efa's hats. A flurry of books come flying towards us, closely followed by tonight's supper.

Everyone steps back from the house, unable to tear their eyes from the astonishing spectacle. A brisk breeze begins to whip around us, snatching musical scores from shaking hands, tossing them into the air and scattering them across the grass like blossom.

Stones continue to tumble until the walls of my house are no more and are replaced by a bulbous cloud of dust and smoke. And, as the dust finally settles, what has been lying beneath and within my house for centuries is revealed.

In place of the top of the tower is the head of a dragon.

In place of our main living quarters is a long, broad, ridged body.

The dragon slowly turns her head and looks at us through narrow yellow eyes.

She carefully lifts each leg in turn, pulling them from their shackles with ease, as if testing them for strength, her eyes not leaving us.

No one dares to move.

I glance at Emrys and Medwyn and they look back at me.

What have we unleashed?

The creature towers above us, small plumes of smoke floating down like little storm clouds from her flaring nostrils.

I barely dare open my mouth, terrified of drawing the creature's attention to me.

I realise I hadn't for a moment considered what she might look like if we released her. How huge she would be. I absorb every detail of her peculiar, terrifying body: the sharp-looking spines that begin on the top of her head and end at the tip of her tail, the intricate arrangement of tarnished gold scales, the razor-like claws, her raw, sore-looking belly.

Muscles ripple under her jaw as her gaze sweeps across us. She thrashes her tail from side to side, sweeping up a candelabra, a moose head and a small display cabinet, sending them flying through the air towards the ice house.

A familiar stooped figure emerges through the settling dust.

It's one of the Aireys. He's clutching a long spear-like stick in bony fingers. As I glance about I realise that some of the singers must have run off in the chaos to arm themselves. Groups of men are now creeping across the lawn towards the dragon, wielding rakes and hoes and anything they can get their hands on. At least two are carrying shotguns.

"Don't hurt her!" I scream, sprinting past them, positioning myself between them and the dragon. "She won't touch you!" Despite her appearance, I'm certain she's more frightened than any of us.

But still the crowd of men edge towards me and the dragon, forcing me to step backwards towards her. I know most of them. They were in the church that night.

A sudden movement in the ground forces me to spin

round to face the dragon. She's rising up unsteadily to her full height, revealing the extent of the damage to her belly. And through the gap beneath her appear both Aireys, in black frock coats and top hats, carrying long lethal-looking sticks. The dragon takes a tentative step away from them towards me, the crowd and the sea behind us. Everyone takes a step back. I remain between them and the dragon, my eyes searching for Emrys and Medwyn.

Some of the men bark commands to each other and run round the dragon like sheepdogs. Recoiling from them, she lumbers on towards me and the sea.

Medwyn appears through the crowd, followed by Emrys. "She can't go into the sea!" he screams. "The water will douse her flames. It will kill her."

I run to the dragon and stand in front of her face, my heart thundering. She looks down at me through narrow, unblinking eyes, her breath hot and heavy on my cheeks. She lowers her head towards me, her eyes fixed on mine. She opens her mouth slightly, only an inch or two, but it is enough for me to note the long rows of razor-like teeth and a bright, orange-red glow coming from deep within her throat. Smoky tendrils slip from her nostrils and curl towards me like slim, beckoning fingers.

She seems to be considering me, perhaps working out who or what I am. I hold my breath, not daring to draw my eyes from hers, trying not to inhale her hot, acrid breath.

Everyone falls silent, but out of the corner of my eye I'm aware of an Airey slipping silently towards us.

I reach up and touch the dragon's jagged cheek. Medwyn and Emrys place themselves, like sentinels, on either side of her, whispering to her in the way they did when she was still trapped.

"You have to fly," I shout. "It's the only way." I point to the sky and flap my arms up and down. She puts her head on one side as if contemplating what I just said.

A sudden shout from the crowd makes me spin round.

Pa is racing towards me. "Wren, it'll incinerate you! What are you thinking?" he shrieks.

"She won't hurt me," I hiss. "Can't you see how frightened she is?"

Pa grabs my arm and tries to pull me away, but I shake him off.

"She needs to fly, Pa!" I shout. "We should be protecting her, not mining her, like she's some sort of mountain!" I'm almost spitting now I'm so angry with him all over again. "She needs to be free, can't you see that? Away from people like you and the Aireys, who only want to hurt her. We have to help her fly!"

"I don't think she can, Wren. She's too weak," Medwyn says quietly.

"Maybe she just doesn't know what to do," I say.

"Perhaps one of us could show her." Medwyn says, looking at me pointedly. He's almost unrecognisable, with cheeks and hair coated in dust.

The Aireys stand like a pair of crows, their coat tails flapping, hollow eyes watching us, listening to our conversation, calculating their next move. I glance at the crowd, at our neighbours and friends – momentarily still, a garden of statues, weapons nervously held high. But I sense the mood is changing.

Perhaps noticing this too, one of the Aireys shrieks at them. "If you don't kill it, it'll kill us all. You saw what it did to the house! It'll do the same to your houses if you let it live. Drive the beast into the sea!"

A collective rumble of distrust comes from the crowd.

"And look at all that gold," the other shouts, waving his stick at one of the dragon's flanks. "It's worth a king's ransom. Slay that beast and you'll be rich forever."

"It's a she," I hiss at them under my breath.

The group of men closest to us look hungrily at the dragon's scales, and then at the Aireys with suspicious eyes.

"We need to help her!" I shout to the crowd, wishing I had a bigger voice. "She can't go in the sea – it'll kill her!"

The dragon suddenly lurches sideways as an Airey delivers a blow to her exposed underbelly with his stick.

She takes another tentative step away from him and towards the sea. I stay close to her, reassuring her, imploring her to fly, but even if she does understand me, she simply doesn't know what to do.

"Can we get everyone to sing again? Would that help her fly?" I say to Medwyn.

"We could try," he says, running his fingers through his hair in despair. "I thought getting the mountains to call her would have roused her to fly. But clearly it wasn't enough."

As if Pa has finally listened to me, he yanks a garden fork out of a nearby rose bed and points it at the Aireys. "You stay away from that dragon," he hisses. "And my daughter!"

"Yes, you stay away from my sister," Tudur shouts, squaring up to the Airey, balling his fists.

I look at him in astonishment. "Thank you," I say.

He nods.

A distant toot-toot drags my attention from Pa and I spin round to see Aunty Efa charging down the lawn towards me, flanked by Gelert and Pelham. She's shouting something to me, beckoning me to join her.

"Go!" Pa says. "I'll stay here."

"Don't let them hurt her, and keep her out of the water!" I shout at him before sprinting up the lawn towards Aunty Efa. She's already spinning her wheelchair round and yells at me to jump aboard.

"I have a plan!" she shouts, grinning.

I leap up on to her coal scuttle and wrap my arms round her shoulders as she chugs at speed towards the yard at the back of the house.

We skid to a halt outside the workshop. "I've been a bit busy," she says, looking pleased with herself, "with a rather important project."

I leap off her wheelchair, my heart pounding, almost not daring to imagine what she's talking about, but my heart still bursting with hope.

"I know how much the Phoenix meant to you," she says. "I've been repairing it in secret; I didn't want your pa to find out and try to stop me. And then when I heard about that poor creature, I wondered if it might actually be useful, rather than just a death trap!"

I stare at her, trying to absorb what she's telling me. My eyes fill with tears as memories of the crash come flooding back.

"I can't," I whisper. "I'm not a bird. I know that now."

"Oh, poppycock, of course you can!"

My stomach somersaults at the thought of trying to fly again. "But last time I just ruined everything, Aunty Efa," I cry. "I'm just a too-small girl with stupid, oversized ideas. Pa's right. I have to rein myself in. I know that now."

Aunty Efa takes my hand in hers. "You are nothing of the sort," she says. "You are Wren, and you have an imagination as vast as Snowdonia. That's what makes you who you are."

"But I can't help her," I wail. "I don't know how to fly! Last time I got it all wrong, and look what happened."

"But you did fly, didn't you? You flew over the house and above the water."

"Until I fell out of the sky."

"Well, I've made a few tweaks to the design, which means that shouldn't happen again. Wren, you are your mother's daughter. You have daredevil blood pulsing through your veins, not the remnants of some silly man who died hundreds of years ago. So, come along. You, my girl, need to teach our dragon how to fly."

She chugs into the workshop and I follow her in.

I gasp. Before us is the Phoenix, fully restored, and looking even more resplendent than it did before the accident. Aunty Efa's favourite red dress has been used to cover part of one of the wings, replacing one that must have been too damaged to re-use. My eyes fill with tears. Aunty Efa rests a hand on my arm. "I hope you don't mind, but I've added a few extra flourishes," she says, pointing towards a double layer of feathers in shades of red and gold.

I swallow the lump in my throat and squeeze her hand.

"And now you have a dragon to save," she says, "so what are you waiting for? Oh, and you'll need these." She tosses me a pair of protective glasses, similar to the ones Medwyn made, but with fat rubbery rims round the lenses.

I grin at her and haul open the concertina workshop doors, and together we tow the Phoenix out of the workshop. We attach it with a length of rope to the back of the wheelchair and I leap into my coracle, quickly refamiliarising myself with the controls. Everything has been repaired and looks even better than it did before. I hadn't realised Aunty Efa was so skilled. My hands are shaking, but from the excitement of what we're about to do rather than fear.

Aunty Efa tips a little coal from her scuttle into her furnace and we chug through the yard towards the garden, the dogs still flanking the wheelchair.

"The tide's in," I shout, my heart sinking. "We won't be able to take off from St Tysilio's!"

"We'll just have to make do with the garden!" Aunty Efa calls back to me, her wild, red hair spiralling above her head, her emerald skirts swirling about her legs. "I have a bit of that daredevil blood in me too, remember!"

And with that she accelerates hard past the side of the house, down the lawn and towards the crowd, and the dragon. It's on the beach now, and only two or three feet from the water.

The crowd are keeping their distance from the dragon and there are only a handful of people waving weapons at it now, but the Aireys are still there, forcing it on towards the water.

"Hold tight!" Aunty Efa shouts.

I pull my protective glasses over my eyes.

We hurtle towards the sea; I had no idea her wheelchair could go so fast! She shouts at everyone to get out of our way, tooting her horn over and over. I bounce about behind her, over the bumpy lawn, gripping the sides of the coracle, my teeth clacking, my heart pumping with exhilaration.

The crowd, seeing us tearing towards them, scatter in all directions, and even the Aireys throw their long, brittle bodies to the ground.

The distance between us and the dragon is closing rapidly. My coracle begins to shudder as the air begins to force the wings up, and, recognising the sensation, I grab hold of the rope, ready to detach myself from Aunty Efa's wheelchair.

And then, just like last time, the magic happens. The wings begin to tremble, signalling their readiness to fly. I throw the rope over the side. The wind rushes beneath me, and I lift up and up into the air, just clearing the heads of the crowd, an ashen-faced Pa, a grinning Tudur and the dragon.

I rise sharply, my heart soaring, up over the waters of the strait, rising steeply until the people on the beach are little more than toy soldiers far below. I make a steep turn and head back towards the dragon. I mustn't frighten her. I decide to stay high and fly past to show her how it's done. Maybe there's something deep within her that will know what to do once she's seen *me* soaring through the air like a bird.

I tug on the cord that controls the tail and lower the Phoenix just a little, and fly past her, not more than twenty feet above her spiny back. She looks up at me with interest but is distracted by another sharp prod from one of the Aireys who has picked himself up from the ground and renewed his attempt to drive her into the water.

I wait until I've gained enough height again before making another steep turn and swoop back once more towards the dragon.

The sun is beginning to sink, slowly transforming the sky from wispy blue to deep crimson.

A collective gasp from below makes me twist round to see what's happening on the ground. As the sky changes hue, so too do the scales on the dragon's back, turning from dusty gold to a shimmering red.

One of the Aireys gives her another sharp prod with his stick. The dragon looks at him, as if coming to her senses for the first time since her release. She slowly turns round, lifts one of her giant legs, scoops up the Airey and hurls him towards the water. He shoots up into the sky and for one terrifying moment I think he might collide with me as I thunder past, but I miss him and he lands with a satisfying splash in deep water halfway across the strait.

The dragon's colour is now so vibrant, her body seems to be on fire.

I call out as I approach her. "Follow me!"

I catch sight of Pa and Tudur. They're shepherding the singing groups into one large ensemble. Bar one or two, their weapons have been abandoned, tossed into a pile on the beach. Medwyn stands between the dragon and a stick-waving Airey. Emrys is close by her side, whispering to her.

And then the people of Anglesey burst into song again. First the sopranos, then the tenors and finally the basses – deep growly voices that rumble across the water like thunder. I take another turn, and as I fly past again I'm enveloped in a cacophony of song that sweeps towards the mountains, inviting them, forcing them to respond one final time. And as the voices swell in a crescendo of sound, the dragon hesitantly lifts her wings.

The choirs step back away from her.

I hear Pa shout at them to keep singing.

I head towards the setting sun, then turn again and fly as close as I dare to the dragon. Our eyes meet. "Follow me!" I shout. "You can do this! You are brilliant and strong!"

A giant boom shakes the ground. The Phoenix trembles. Waves crash on to the beach. The boom comes again, deep and low and long, sending a ripple of fear through my heart. I take a deep breath and swoop once more towards the dragon.

She lifts her wings, still watching me, and slowly she rises into the air. I take a small turn and head off towards the mountains, aware of her hot breath on my back. And, as if swept along by the voices, we fly together towards the mountains.

After a while, she comes to my side, her eyes set on the tall peaks rising ahead of us.

She opens her enormous jaws and belches a plume of flame that consumes the air around us, singeing my wing tip and incinerating a few ostrich feathers.

We fly together above the mountains, over the place she began her life as a small, hot, abandoned egg. Together we soar, rising and falling like birds. She is finally free, and so, I realise, am I. I'm not a proper daredevil like Ma, but there's a feeling within me I can't resist. The need to fly. To rise above the world. To soar.

We encircle the mountaintops for a while, as the dragon, like me, learns to use her wings.

The sun is setting now. Night is creeping towards us.

The time has come to say farewell.

"Goodbye!" I shout.

She lets out a huge roar and the mountains bellow in response. She is home, and I must leave her to live her life above the world, watching over us from a safe distance.

With a heavy heart I waggle my wings and wave farewell. She nods, and with a flick of her tail is gone.

I turn round and head home, my heart heavy.

I fly low along the Menai Strait, under the arches of the bridge, skimming the waves like a gull. People are stretched out along the shore, some holding hands, some waving, others scratching their heads as if not quite believing what they just saw. I lower the Phoenix, my strange, ramshackle collection of bits and bobs that somehow took me up into the sky and allowed me to fly, slowly losing height until my coracle is just inches from the water. I hold her steady, keeping her wings up and level.

The hull of the Phoenix, my coracle, gently touches the water and I come to a gradual halt. I remove my glasses and tie them round my wrist.

Medwyn and Pa set off from the shore in a rowing boat to bring me home. Someone else has come out in a fishing boat to drag a bedraggled and furious-looking Airey from the water.

We stand together, Pa, Aunty Efa, Tudur and me, looking down into the smoking pit that was once our home.

"Are you still furious with me?" I say to Pa. "For all this?"

"Of course not," he says. "You're a better person than me, Wren."

"I did destroy our house," I whisper.

"But perhaps we didn't need such a monster of a house." He walks over to the dragon painting, now lying in a mangled heap on the ground, and picks it up, examining it, turning it over. Eventually he tosses it into the pit.

I feel a warm hand slip into mine. I look down, assuming it's Aunty Efa, but her hands are folded together on her knee. The warmth remains for just a moment before slipping away as if it was never there.

Epilogue

Pentref Airfield, Anglesey, November 1936
(Sixty-six years later)

She arrives on her bicycle, as she does most weeks when the weather is fair, and dismounts with the agility of someone years younger, her belly fizzing with excitement. She wheels her well-worn Elswick towards the hangar and leans it in its usual place, under the overhanging eaves where it will stay dry should it rain. She squints at the sky through periwinkle eyes framed by slim, translucent scars, the marks of a life well lived.

Her sight is as razor-sharp as it ever was.

Tomos appears out of his workshop, wiping his oily hands on a rag. "She's all ready for you," he says. "Looks like a good day for flying."

She nods in thanks and disappears into the small room at the back of the hangar where she changes quickly into her flying suit. The leather is stiff from age and the cold, but it slips easily over her tiny frame. She pulls on her boots and straps her parachute to her back, securing it carefully round her shoulders and waist. Finally she eases her flying helmet down over her fine, white hair, and slides a stray strand back up under the leather. Wrapping her goggles round her wrist, she goes out to her Cirrus Moth.

The sight of her biplane never ceases to take her breath away. She walks round it, running her fingers along the fuselage, doing the usual checks, even though she knows Tomos will have done them already. She's never come to terms with her extravagance at buying such a machine, but from the moment she first set eyes on it she was in love. And with its open cockpit she'd known straight away it would be perfect for her needs.

Certain everything is as it should be, and that the fuel tank is full, she takes hold of the strut over the back of the left wing and leaps up on to it. She stands on the wing, scanning the sky, her heart full of hope, before climbing into the rear cockpit.

The weather is perfect, the sky a pale winter blue, and clear apart from a few distant, fluffy clouds.

Tomos stands in front of the aeroplane, ready to spin the propeller. Wren flicks the ignition switch and shouts, "Contact!" He swings the propeller and leaps back as it settles into a rotation so fast it becomes almost invisible. The engine coughs and splutters a few times but is soon purring like a cat.

She checks the dials. When she is certain everything is in order, she pulls her goggles on and waves to Tomos. He kicks the chocks away, and she begins to trundle towards the grass strip. She pushes the rudder pedals left then right and zigzags towards the runway. As soon as she reaches the runway's threshold, she shuffles back in her seat and clicks the buckles on her harness into place. Underneath her flying suit, her heart is beating like a drum.

She pulls the control stick towards her, and is soon racing along the runway, a smile stretched across her cheeks.

The wheels leave the tarmac and Wren soars up into the air like a bird.

As she rises into the sky, Anglesey, and the mountains,

lakes and forests of North Wales, shrink beneath her. She flies over the Llyn Peninsula, and down over the slate-grey waters of Cardigan Bay, the huge expanse of sea that stretches almost the length of Wales. As always her eyes search the sky above and below and to the left and the right.

Like she often does, she imagines her ma, who didn't get to grow old like her, sitting in the empty front cockpit. Some days she thinks she sees her out on one of the wings, her hair wild, waving at her.

When she reaches the town of Cardigan, she heads inland and flies north again, keeping a safe distance above the Cambrian Mountains; they're white-capped now it's winter, and their dramatic peaks remind her of her aunt's flamboyant hairstyles that lasted well into her old age. Aunty Efa lived to ninety-six. She and Pa remained together for the rest of their lives, squabbling most days over Efa's smuts and Pa's pickiness, but underneath it all they were friends, despite what Pa had done to the dragon. They saw out their years in a small villa overlooking the sea, built out of stone from the old house. Pa often commented on how much he preferred it to the great rambling beast of a house they'd lived in before.

On a whim Wren crosses back over the water and

heads towards the site of the old house, pushing her stick forward to fly low over it. The pit, once prison to a sleeping dragon, remains an open wound in the landscape. It's a tourist attraction now, with a picket fence running round its perimeter, and rope ladders dangling into its depths for the use of more intrepid tourists. The ice house has been reclaimed by nature and from above looks little more than a grassy mound. Wren often wonders what happened to Emrys. He simply slipped away the day after everything happened and was never seen again.

She flies over her little house, next door to the school she taught at for fifty years, teaching girls and boys about mechanics and mathematics, paid for by her pa's profits from his gold-mining activities. He was cleared of theft as it was ruled that technically the dragon was on his land and therefore belonged to him, but many on the island thought that was a terrible miscarriage of justice, and he was forced to make amends by building the school. The Aireys, found guilty of blackmailing Pa after he'd told them about the dragon, lived out the rest of their lives in Beaumaris Gaol, in the old wing in which they used to imprison young women with spirit. Wren notices a slipped slate tile on the school's roof and makes a mental note to go up and repair it when she has a moment. Tudur comes up to see her from time to time. He went to Oxford to study the classics and remained there, eventually becoming a professor of Greek literature. He's not quite as pompous as he was when he was ten, and his visits are only ever brief, so they get on pretty well these days.

Wren makes a tight turn, shoots up into the air and flies back across the sparkling water towards the mountains, heading to the place she said farewell to the dragon. She was out on the water just this morning in her coracle. Medwyn and their daughters are forever worrying about her taking it near the Swellies at her age, so she'd slipped out early before anyone was up. Her eyes sweep the horizon, searching for a flash of red. She taps her fuel gauge, sighing as the needle dips. She does some quick calculations in her head, needing to be certain she has enough fuel to return safely to the airfield.

A flash of something to the right catches her eye and she heads towards it. Her heart pounds in the way it always does whenever she thinks she might be close to finding what she's spent the last sixty-six years searching for.

Something definitely feels different about the air. A slight warmth on her back. Perhaps it's just the sun making a rare appearance. She glances behind her but sees nothing of interest. She scans her instruments again to check that all is well with her aeroplane.

But the heat comes again, immersing her in its warm embrace. A flash of red swoops past. Wren's heart begins to thunder. The control stick quivers in her shaking hands.

And then, like a miracle, the beast that was once trapped beneath her house appears by her side – a vast creature of red and gold and orange, sparkling like a giant jewel in the afternoon sun, her scales seeming to be on fire. She flies alongside Wren, her narrow yellow eyes scanning her. Wren waves a shaking hand in greeting.

And, as if suddenly recognising her, the dragon flicks her tail and soars up above Wren's little plane and loops round her like a puppy. Wren notes with satisfaction how much she's grown in the last sixty-six years, and that her belly is now covered in a protective pattern of red-gold scales. She holds her plane steady as the dragon soars and dives by her side. She realises she's smiling, a smile so wide it makes her cheeks ache.

She pulls back hard on the stick and shoots up towards the clouds. The dragon rises with her, and they fly together, up and up into the sky, before plunging at breakneck speed back down towards the mountains, then soaring once more over Cardigan Bay just as it turns to a deep, flame red. Together they swoop and rise and dive, as free as birds. With the weight lifted from her old bones, Wren feels like a child again.

The dragon stays close by her side as she heads back up to Anglesey. When they reach the Menai Strait, the dragon inclines her head as if saying a final farewell. She flicks her enormous tail and with a seemingly impossible burst of speed soars up into the sky and is gone.

Wren is all alone in an empty sky.

She flies back to the airfield, not caring much if she runs out of fuel. In a rare moment of recklessness, she turns round to take one final spin over the mountains, and as she looks down she notices that the landscape below, with its mountain ridges, crags and deep lakes, gives the impression of a curled-up dragon. For one fanciful moment Wren imagines Wales as one giant dragon, perhaps even the mother of her dragon. She wonders if there are other young ones still down there, buried deep beneath its ridges, still sleeping, preparing to rise when the time is just right.

Wren lands her aeroplane with ease and trundles back along the runway towards the hangar. When she comes to a stop, she removes her goggles, climbs out of the cockpit, jumps lightly on to the wing and then on to the hardstanding in front of the hangar. She returns to the little room at the back, slips out of her flying suit, hangs her goggles on the hook and walks out of the building for the last time.

Glossary

Understanding the ancient Welsh naming system

For hundreds of years, many families in Wales followed a patronymic naming system in which a son was given his father's, grandfather's and even great-grandfather's names as his surname using "ap" or "ab" (a contraction of the Welsh word "mab", or "map" in Old Welsh, meaning son) to connect these names. So Gruffudd ap Bleddyn ap Llewelyn literally means Gruffudd, son of Bleddyn, son of Llewelyn. Some names were even longer than this, with five, six or seven family names all linked together. Women were also known by their father's and grandfather's names, but used "ferch" or "verch", which means "daughter of". Fixed surnames were adopted from the sixteenth century onwards.

The age of early flight and the concept of lift

Wren's design for the Phoenix was inspired by the work of French sea captain Jean-Marie Le Bris, who built a glider, the *L'Albatros artificiel*, in 1856. His flying machine was placed on a cart towed by a horse, and he lifted up from the beach at Sainte-Anne-la-Palud, Finistère. It's reported he flew to a height of 100 metres and for a distance of 200 metres. This is believed to be the first ever flight where the craft flew higher than its point of departure – i.e. not as a result of someone jumping off a tall building and gliding or tumbling to the ground!

Like Wren, Le Bris was fascinated by the idea of flight. He was the first to identify the concept of "aspiration", now known as "lift". Lift is achieved in part by the design of an aeroplane's wing. If the shape is just right, air will move faster over the curved upper surface of the wing than it does along the flat underside of the wing. The faster moving air produces less pressure than the slower moving air, causing the wing to lift towards the area of low pressure.

I don't know if Le Bris would have been the type to write to a twelve-year-old girl in North Wales who dreamed of flying, explaining how he built his artificial bird, but I like to think he might have been tempted!

Acknowledgements

Eternal thanks to Kirsty Stansfield at Nosy Crow for your enthusiasm, insight and encouragement as Wren's strange story fluttered from the darkest recesses of my brain on to the page. Your trust in me to find the story meant everything, as I didn't have quite the same faith in myself! Thank you to illustrator extraordinaire, David Dean, and cover designer Nicola Theobald for creating a cover that makes my heart sing. And to all the PR, marketing and sales gurus at Nosy Crow – Wren wouldn't be landing in readers' hands without all your hard work, so thank you all!

To my amazing agent, Joanna Moult, thank you for taking the time to talk through my story ideas and for your wisdom on writing and life beyond.

Huge thanks to Stephen Rees at Bangor University for talking to me about the history of song in Wales, and for introducing me to Penillion and Plygain singing. If I have made any errors in my descriptions of music and song, the fault is entirely mine.

Thank you to my MA in Writing for Young People friends and former students, but particularly to the Write Sisters, Anna Crowe, Anne Manson, Sarah Stevens and Andrea Fowkes. Thank you for your enthusiasm for

Wren when it was just a fledgling idea, and for your constant friendship and inspiring writing chats.

To Alex Evelyn and Alex Cotter, for the coffees and writing chats, and for being smashing, insightful friends. To Team Skylark for the hilarious WhatsApp chats, to the Southbank Writers for all the bookish chat and fun London meet-ups, and to the other Nosy Crow authors for your advice and support.

To my fabulous friends, Becky Quew-Jones and Jennie Elderkin for bravely reading the earliest draft of Wren and for your positivity and encouragement.

To my brilliant nephew, Gruff, for allowing me to borrow your name!

To my own long-dead ancestor, my many-greats uncle, Rheinallt ap Gruffudd ap Bleddyn, for being the inspiration behind Wren's many-greats grandfather. Rheinallt was part of the rebel garrison at Harlech that backed Jasper Tudor and the exiled Henry VI in their campaigns against Edward IV – the song "Men of Harlech" was inspired by their daring deeds. Rheinallt did some terrible things to the men of Chester inside the ancient fortified house in which I grew up (and my brother still lives) in North Wales. I no longer live in Wales, but Wren is my love letter to the place I still call home, and the place I hope one day to live again.

To all the pilots in my family, but particularly to my great uncle, Sandy Wynne-Eyton, a pioneering pilot who was one of the first to attempt a solo crossing of the Atlantic in 1930. Growing up hearing stories of his adventures inspired Wren's passion for flying. To his wife, Helen Wynne-Eyton (Silver) a fearless and inspirational woman who learned to fly in 1930 and in the same year flew her small aeroplane from Heston in the south of England to Nairobi!

To my husband, Kev, eternal thanks for your endless enthusiasm and support for my writing, and for being my first reader and sounding block for my plot conundrums. To my children, Hattie and Dylan, for being the most brilliant human beings – I'm so proud of you both. And finally to my dog, Bronte, the best writing buddy any author could hope for.